CONJURE WEB

A Moonshadow Bay Novel, Book 3

YASMINE GALENORN

A Nightqueen Enterprises LLC Publication

Published by Yasmine Galenorn

PO Box 2037, Kirkland WA 98083-2037

CONJURE WEB

A Moonshadow Bay Novel

Copyright © 2021 by Yasmine Galenorn

First Electronic Printing: 2021 Nightqueen Enterprises LLC

First Print Edition: 2021 Nightqueen Enterprises

Cover Art & Design: Ravven

Art Copyright: Yasmine Galenorn

Editor: Elizabeth Flynn

A Nightqueen Enterprises LLC Publication

Published in the United States of America

ACKNOWLEDGMENTS

Welcome to the world of Moonshadow Bay, where magic lurks in the moonlight, and danger in the shadows.

Thanks to my usual crew: Samwise, my husband, Andria and Jennifer—without their help, I'd be swamped. To the women who have helped me find my way in indie, you're all great, and thank you to everyone. To Kate Danley in particular, for running our author sprints that have helped me regain my focus in this current pandemic. To my wonderful cover artist, Ravven, for the beautiful work she's done.

Also, my love to my furbles, who keep me happy. My most reverent devotion to Mielikki, Tapio, Ukko, Rauni, and Brighid, my spiritual guardians and guides. My love and reverence to Herne, and Cernunnos, and to the Fae, who still rule the wild places of this world. And a nod to the Wild Hunt, which runs deep in my magick, as well as in my fiction.

You can find me through my website at Galenorn.com and be sure to sign up for my newsletter to keep updated on all my latest releases! You can find my advice on writing, discussions about the books, and general ramblings on my YouTube channel. If you liked this book, I'd be grateful if you'd leave a review—it helps more than you can think.

March, 2021
Brightest Blessings,
~The Painted Panther~
~Yasmine Galenorn~

WELCOME TO CONJURE WEB

Moonshadow Bay...where magic lurks in the moonlight, and danger hides in the shadows.

As January faces the Aseer to find out what her magical strengths are, she also delves into her family history, where she discovers dark secrets about her great-grandmother Colleen and a long-lost child. But when she and Ari take on a private case, they find themselves in over their heads. They must ask Conjure Ink for help in solving a riddle when a mother insists that her child isn't really her child. January's investigation leads everyone down the rabbit hole of magical intrigue and into the world of the Woodlings, where January finds her world-view of what is actually real changing, even as it puts her life in danger.

Reading Order for the Moonshadow Bay Series:

- Book 1: Starlight Web
- Book 2: Midnight Web
- Book 3: Conjure Web

CHAPTER ONE

"*I* refuse to be married in white," Ari said. "I simply *won't* wear a white dress. Neither will Meagan. We aren't virgins, we're both forty, and we aren't even *straight*. Nobody's giving away anything that hasn't already been out the barn door and around the track. Since we're getting married in summer, I want to wear purple and she's wearing green."

I suppressed a laugh and just nodded. Ari and I were flipping through bridal magazines, looking at dresses. She and Meagan were getting married on July 12, and that gave us five months to get everything ready. Since Meagan's parents refused to take part in their daughter's big, magical gay wedding, we were coming up with cost-saving ideas that would be beautiful, as well.

"So, do you have a theme yet?" I asked, picking up another sandwich and biting into it. We were eating lunch on my back porch. Even though it was still chilly—it was a rainy 58 degrees—we both were more than ready for some fresh air and sunshine. The fresh air, we had. The sunshine, not so much.

"We're thinking of a wisteria garden party theme... Meagan wants a tea instead of a dinner, and I like that idea. Oh, hey, that brings me to another question. Can we hold the wedding in your backyard?" Ari tossed the magazine to the side and picked up another one, starting to leaf through it. "None of these is right. I haven't seen a dress I like."

"Of course you can. Hold the wedding here, that is. And may I suggest that you look at ball gowns? I know it's not the typical thing, but most of them are more colorful than wedding dresses, and usually a lot prettier. I bet you could find something in that direction." I set down *The Mature Bride*, which was a magazine that focused on women over thirty who were getting married. Ari and Meagan, like me, were well over that. "Honestly, thirty is not old. Hell, I'm forty-one and I don't even feel that old—just…a little seasoned."

As I focused on my lunch, a gust of fresh air whistled past. The wind was coming in off the Salish Sea, and the sound of birdsong echoed from tree to tree. We were due for rain again, but the ground smelled like it was waking up, and I could feel the rhythms of the earth shift and turn as the equinox drew near. We were headed for Ostara, the spring celebration of balance and new beginnings, and everywhere, I could see the signs that the world was preparing to grow and stretch out, like a rose whose petals were unfolding.

"That's a good idea. I'll run the idea by Meagan and we'll look online. We'd rather spend the bulk of our money on a fabulous party and honeymoon than on the dresses and flowers. Though I insist on having wisteria there, and black roses—well, the ones that look black." She took a long sip of her coffee.

"What does Meagan want?" I finished my ham sandwich and leaned back, sipping my mocha.

"She's left the flowers up to me. In exchange, she gets to pick our first dance song. We're both writing our own vows, and we both are agreeing on the menu for the tea and the cake. I wanted chocolate, she wanted tres leches, so we compromised on a chocolate-caramel cake." She shook her head, grinning. "I never thought I'd be planning a wedding. I really didn't believe that I'd ever meet anybody I could get along with enough to commit to."

At first, when I realized that Ari and Meagan were serious, I had a spate of jealousy, worrying that I might lose my best friend. But Meagan—whom I had loathed in high school—had turned out to be a decent adult once she came out of the closet. I no longer worried about that. It occurred to me that Ari might have felt the same way when I had gotten married to Ellison, and I felt embarrassed that I had pulled away from her for so many years, thanks to Ellison's dislike of all things magical. With me and my best friend both being witches, he really got his nose out of joint when she came to visit. Meagan actually welcomed me in like a sister.

"Well, you picked a winner," I said. "And you know I'd say something if I didn't believe that."

"I know—you sure did when you first found out who she was. No more 'Mean Meagan,' right?" Ari laughed.

"Right," I said, rolling my eyes. "I'm sorry I was so whiny about her."

3

"Well, she was a piece of work back in high school. So, are you ready to tackle your attic?"

I nodded, staring into my coffee mug morosely. "Yeah. But the caffeine's done."

"Get your butt out of the chair, January. We can have more when we're done," she said with a laugh. "Dangle *that* carrot in front of you."

I grumbled but picked up my dishes. Ari gathered her things and we headed back inside as the clouds broke and a huge deluge came gushing down from the sky. Grateful that the porch was enclosed, I took one last deep breath of the air that hung heavy with the scents of cedar and fir, of geosim and pungent earth, and we headed inside to clean out the attic.

WHEN I MOVED BACK TO MOONSHADOW BAY AFTER inheriting my parents' house, I had changed out some of the furniture for my own, and I had finally faced reality and gone through the closets and cleared out my mother's and father's clothing. It had been hard—I still missed them dreadfully—but it was time, and I needed the space. But I'd left the attic alone. Now, it was time to tackle whatever was up there. Ari had agreed to help me.

The attic was accessible through a trap door in the hallway ceiling outside the master bedroom. I carried a stepstool up to the second floor so that I could catch hold of the ring attached to the trap door. As the door opened, a retractable set of stairs eased down. They appeared flimsy, but my father—who had been something of a handyman—had reinforced them so they were strong and sturdy. He had also affixed a locking mechanism to the bottom stair so the steps couldn't jog loose and fold up when someone was on them.

I moved the stepstool and flipped on the light to the attic. The switch was located on the wall beneath the attic, and that made it possible to see as we headed up the steps. My father had been a practical man and had made life as easy as he could for my mother and himself.

I glanced at Ari. "Ready?"

She nodded. She was carrying a broom and a wet-mop. I was armed with a duster and a box of heavy-duty garbage bags. "And able."

"Then onward, Wheeler!" I pointed to the stairs. "You first."

"You just want me to make sure there aren't any spiders hanging out at the top."

"You know me well," I said, laughing. I wasn't arachno-phobic, but I wasn't that fond of the little buggers. I loved snakes, but spiders were not my favorite creatures.

The attic was well-kept. My mother had deep cleaned the house from top to bottom twice a year, so even though there was dust and a few cobwebs, and an occasional spider web, it wasn't the attic from a horror movie. In fact, it was rather cozy. My father had tiled the floor, saying that, should the roof ever leak, no hardwoods or carpet would get ruined or spawn mold. The large room was finished, and my mother had painted the walls a creamy white to bring in more light through the windows on either end. The attic was almost the size of the second story.

One side was used for storage, and my mother had turned the other side into a crafting sanctuary. While she had kept her magical supplies in the library for easy access, she stored all her fabric and yarn and scrap-booking supplies in the attic. There was also a long folding table and several chairs, along with a very bright LED lamp. There was also a TV up here. I had only been back in Moonshadow Bay three months, and as I said, I had left the attic alone during that time.

"Wow, your parents really made use of this space," Ari said.

"Yeah, they did. While I was growing up, the attic was pretty much beams and wood and insulation. But about ten years ago, my father got the renovation bug and my mother told me they were going to 'optimize' their use of the house. They must have redone the attic at that point, because I know that with the last set of renovations, they focused on the downstairs and their master bath."

I looked around, suddenly feeling melancholy. There were signs of my mother everywhere—in the silk flowers that graced the sideboard, in the delicate lace curtains on the windows, in the protection charms that hung on the walls. I wondered if my father had ever felt the urge to join her up here. He thought he was from a weak magical line, but since he actually had a strong witchblood heritage, I wondered if he had ever felt compelled to work with magic. Given he had no clue that Rowan Firesong—the strongest and oldest witch in town—was his mother, I doubted that he had ever been to the Aseer.

"What are you thinking about?" Ari asked.

"The fact that Rowan Firesong is my grandmother," I said. "I wonder whether my father ever questioned his lineage. He had to feel the energy my mother worked with

—it was in his blood. So why didn't he ever question his roots?"

"Maybe he did, but he never told you," Ari said, looking around. "Where do you want to start?"

"I guess the craft cabinets. I'm about as handy with a needle and thread as I am with a chain saw. Which is to say, *Stand back, the woman is dangerous*." I sighed, opening the first cabinet. There were stacks of neatly folded fabric remnants and yardage. While some of it was pretty, I knew I'd never use most of it. There was also a pile of empty charm bags. Those I would keep. I decided that I could probably sew a straight line, so I would keep the stack of precut squares that sat next to the bags. Everything else, except for the thread and basic sewing tools, went into one of the garbage bags.

"What about the yarn? This is good quality and might come in handy for knot magic," Ari said, holding up one of the skeins.

I shrugged. "Yes, but I don't need two shelves of it. Keep one of each of the basic colors—and two of black, red, and white. The rest can go. I'll keep all the embroidery thread, that can be used in so many charms. But the patterns can go. I'll never sew a dress, my mother was skinnier than I was, and I don't entertain any desire to turn into Suzy Seamstress any time soon."

We moved on to the next cabinet. I kept the modeling clay, but opted to get rid of the papier-mâché strips. I kept all of the blank wooden plaques and paints—they looked like fun and I liked to paint at times—and the sketchbooks. I also kept the rotary tool, and a wood burner and the glue guns.

7

"I guess I'm keeping more than I thought," I said. "I can see a use for a number of these things."

"I can too, and you can always get rid of them later, if you find you don't use them." Ari carried the bag of material and other goodies I was donating over to the stairway and dropped it down to the floor below. "All right, the storage side. That will take more time, given there are a number of trunks and boxes there."

I grimaced. "Right. We may have to ask Killian to come carry things down if they're too heavy. Okay, let's dive in."

The storage area contained at least ten trunks and several pieces of furniture. I eyed the two standing lamps that were in front of the boxes. Neither was my style, and I picked up one.

"These go. Both of them."

We carried them over to an empty area in the large room and set them to one side. There were also several chairs and a small table. The table was one of those with a built-in chessboard and drawers that held the pieces. And the drawers had beautiful silver pieces inside. I smiled.

"This was my father's. He and I used to play every weekend. I want to find a place for it downstairs."

"I remember that—you used to rope me into playing with you. I never told you how much I hated the game because I knew you loved it," Ari said.

I stared at her. "Why didn't you say anything? I loved playing but I never wanted to rope you into doing something you didn't like!"

"You just seemed so geeked out about it. But I'll play backgammon with you any day!"

"You've met your match. I used to play backgammon

with my dorm neighbor every evening while we got stoned," I said, snickering. "I'm a whiz."

"You're a whiz at just about everything," Ari said. "I always envied your brain."

"And I envied your ability to climb a rope. Good grief, remember old lady Krump? She hated me because I just couldn't do what the other girls could. I could barely get up on the balance beam, let alone do a flip on it." I rubbed the top of the chessboard. It was inlaid marble into the oak. "But chess… My father taught me to play when I was five. Every Sunday morning, Mom would make waffles and bacon and sausages…and we would sit and play while we ate. She would paint while we did that. It's one memory I'll never let go of." I drifted off, thinking about my parents. "I'm one of the lucky ones, you know. I had a good childhood. I'll treasure that always."

Ari gave me a quick hug and let out a sigh. "I'm sorry, I know you miss them."

"I do," I said. "I hope they know how much I wish they were still here."

They had died in a car crash not yet a year ago, and I still couldn't get used to the idea that they were both gone. It had been so sudden. The frantic call from my aunt Teran at nine P.M. that my parents were in the hospital, to me speeding up the freeway, praying to every god who would listen that I'd get to the hospital in time and in one piece, to arriving at eleven P.M., only to find my mother crashing just as I got there.

The doctors worked on her frantically as I sat in the hall, numb, unable to speak. She had died before I could say good-bye. My father had already been pronounced brain-dead and I had to make the decision to let him go.

That had been one of the hardest things I had ever had to do.

And all through it, my then-husband kept texting me, asking where to find his good shirt, and why hadn't I asked the maid to clean under the bed—there were dust bunnies there, and had I had the chance to look over the divorce papers and...*ya know*...sign them yet? That was when I first started getting my voice back—when I texted back that I was done being his servant, he could sweep the fucking floor himself, and I'd sign them when I signed them.

Your mother knows how you feel and remember, she is here with us. She watches over you as best as she can. She knows you loved her and your father, Esmara said.

Esmara was one of the Ladies, my ancestors on my mother's side—all strong witch women who came back to guard and guide those of us who were alive. Esmara had been my great-aunt, and she was my personal guardian. My aunt Teran was watched over by Prue, one of Esmara's sisters. I suddenly wondered if my mother had talked to the Ladies while she was alive. It only made sense.

Esmara, who among you watched over my mother?

I did. And so I watch over you, as well.

Tell my mother I miss her. Do you know if my father is still around?

No, love. He's moved on through the Veil.

My mood shifted and I felt unaccountably sad. If he really was gone, I'd never talk to him again. Once someone moved through the Veil, they were usually gone for good. Feeling a little morose, I turned back to the trunks and Ari.

"All right, let's get started on these." I randomly picked one and we set to sorting through the items. Most of the contents consisted of old china and knickknacks that were family mementos. But I also knew that I'd never use most of it, and I hated just packing things away.

"All of this can go," I said, shaking my head. "I'm not keeping stuff I will never use, and that I don't have an attachment to just because they're family history." I paused, picking up a gorgeous perfume bottle. "This, however, I'll keep. I have a feeling I'm going to be starting a perfume bottle collection!"

"You think there's a djinn inside?" Ari asked, grinning.

"I hope not. One was enough." I popped the top and sniffed. "Ooo, whoever wore this, liked spicy perfume." I set it aside. "I wonder how Rameer is doing. I hope he comes back to visit like he said he would." I had freed a djinn trapped in a perfume bottle that I had bought at a thrift store, and after we located his original bottle, he had gone home to his own realm.

"I hope he's okay. I liked him." Ari held up a pair of tarnished silver candlesticks. "What about these?"

"Give away," I said, shaking my head. "I mostly use battery-operated candles due to Xi and Klaus. And when I use actual candles with candle holders, I prefer crystal." My kittens were barely four months old and far too curious. Candles that produced actual flame I reserved for ritual use, and I scrupulously made sure they were extinguished when I was done.

We had worked our way through eight of the ten trunks when I paused, frowning. I looked around. Something felt off, though I couldn't quite put my finger on what it was. I listened, hard, but heard nothing. A glance around the room gave me no clue, but it felt like a shadow had fallen across the afternoon.

"What time is it?"

Ari glanced at her phone. "It's almost four. We've been at it nearly four hours."

"Let's take a break. I'm tired," I said, setting down the crystal bowl I had just found. It was beautiful. "This is pretty," I said, holding it up. A delicate rose pattern wound around the side. "But I have one that's almost identical."

Ari's eyes widened. "That's gorgeous. Meagan would love it."

I handed it to her. "Then give it to her with my regards."

"Are you sure?" She took the crystal bowl, examining it. "This looks old."

"I'm sure. It's lovely, but I doubt if I'd use it."

We headed down the steps, Ari carrying the bowl. At the bottom, there were three big bags of things to give away, not counting everything I was planning to ask Killian to carry down from the attic. I did one last sweep, making sure the kittens hadn't gotten themselves up there when we weren't looking, and closed up the trap door for the time being.

"We'll finish later, just leave the stepstool here," I said, wiping my brow. Even as clean as the attic had been, I felt grungy and dusty.

We stopped in my bathroom to wash our hands and faces, and then headed downstairs for more coffee and a snack. As I pulled shots for the lattes, my mood began to lighten, and I found myself breathing easier. Whatever cloud had sent me into a spiral had vanished, and once again, I relaxed and was able to enjoy the rest of the afternoon, talking to Ari about her wedding plans.

THAT EVENING, KILLIAN AND I RETURNED TO THE ATTIC. He had been working at the clinic all day—he was a veterinarian—and after Ari left, I had made dinner. While he was also my next-door neighbor, we spent at least three to four nights together each week.

"Love, how are you?" he asked, entering the kitchen. We had passed the key-milestone, and had exchanged keys to each other's homes.

"Tired. We made a lot of headway, but I need your help carrying things down from the attic that were too heavy or bulky for Ari and me." I glanced at the oven and set the timer for forty-five minutes. "Lasagna will be ready within the hour, and I made a salad."

"Today's the new moon, don't you have a ritual to perform?"

I shook my head. "I'll meditate later, but I want to get the attic taken care of tonight, if possible."

Killian kissed me on the nose, then motioned for me to follow him. "Let's get busy then."

Killian O'Connell was a bit taller than I was—I was five-nine—and he had curly, shoulder-length light brown hair and emerald green eyes. A small scar on his cheek gave him a slightly roguish look. He told me he had gotten it from treating a wounded lynx for a wildlife conservatory during his early days as a vet. He was muscled but not bulky, and I felt safe around him.

"You really did go through things," he said, staring at

the pile of items I was getting rid of that had been either too large or too delicate to put in the garbage bags.

"Yeah. While you start carrying them down, I think I'll tackle the last two trunks tonight." I glanced around and opened the nearest. To my surprise—and relief—it was empty.

That left a small trunk in the corner, one that had been hidden behind the rest of them. Something about it called to me, and I felt that same wave of uncertainty I had felt earlier. Frowning, I picked up the surprisingly heavy chest and hoisted it over to the crafting table. The chest was about the size of a small footlocker—about two feet long, and fifteen inches both deep and high. It was shaped like an old-fashioned treasure chest, and there was a padlock on it.

"I wonder where the key is for this," I said. I glanced at Killian. "Can you pick the lock?"

"What makes you think I can pick locks at all?" he asked, laughing. "I'm a veterinarian, not a thief."

"You never know what talents someone has unless you ask," I said, grinning. "If you can't pick it, can you bust it?"

He examined the padlock. "Do you have any bolt cutters?"

I thought through what I had seen in the garage. "If I do, they were my father's, and they would be in his work area. Let me go look."

Leaving him with the chest, I dashed down the stairs, then into the kitchen, to the door leading into the garage. Once in the garage, I poked around the tool bench. My father had been extremely organized and I found the bolt cutters right away. They were hanging on the peg board in back of the bench. I grabbed them, along with a crowbar—it seemed like a good idea—and headed back up to the attic.

Killian took the cutters and snapped the padlock as though it were butter. Shifters were incredibly strong, and with the right tool, they could break through a number of things humans couldn't. Or even those of us with witchblood. He set the cutters aside and motioned to me.

"Your chest. You do the honors."

I wrinkled my nose. "Silly man," I said, but I slowly lifted the lid. Most of the chests hadn't been locked, and that this one had been alerted my attention. I felt pulled toward the chest, as though there was something magical inside, or something important that I needed to see.

The first thing I noticed was that there were initials carved on the inside of the lid: *C.O.*

" 'C.O.'? Who's that?" I tried to remember my family history, but nothing stood out. Of course, this might have belonged to someone who wasn't part of the family, but it would be odd that the trunk would be among my parents' belongings.

Inside the trunk, the contents were wrapped in green velvet. The material lined the chest and had been folded over whatever was inside. I cautiously opened the top flaps, only to find myself staring at a dagger in a sheath, a leatherbound book, and a ring. The silver ring had a bear's head on it, and it was exquisitely detailed. The eyes of the bear were inset emeralds, and as I reached for it, a humming made me stop.

"What is it?" Killian asked, craning his neck to see.

"I don't know—there's strong magic in this chest," I said. I picked up the ring out and automatically slid it on my right index finger. It fit perfectly, and I instantly felt a glow of protection and fierceness surround me. Next, I lifted the dagger and slid it out of the leather sheath. The hilt of the dagger was made of bog oak. The hilt fit my hand perfectly, and I raised the blade, which was at least thirteen inches long and made of polished bronze. The dagger sang to me, and I felt something shift as I held it.

"Who owned this?" I whispered.

"Maybe it's in the book?" Killian asked.

The black hand-tooled leather felt smooth under my fingers as I lifted the book out of the chest. I opened the book to the first page and there, in a curving script, I read "Colleen O'Leary Fletcher." I flipped through the pages briefly but I already knew what this was.

"This belonged to my great-grandmother Colleen—who helped found Moonshadow Bay," I said. "This is her dagger, her ring, and her book of shadows." And right then, I knew that I had found a treasure beyond riches.

CHAPTER TWO

*K*illian carried everything downstairs. While he arranged the things I was donating in the garage, I sat at the kitchen table with my great-grandma Colleen's diary, dagger, and ring. Finding them had taken me aback. I wasn't quite sure what to think. Why had my mother kept them locked away instead of using them or displaying them? And it seemed odd that these things had been packed away up in the attic, since Colleen had been one of the founders of Moonshadow Bay, and the items might be better off displayed at the local museum.

But the moment I thought about it, I blew off the idea. That seemed terribly disrespectful, given they were ritual gear.

"Are you going to read it?" Killian asked, returning from the garage. The timer interrupted him and I set the dagger and the book where they wouldn't chance getting splattered. I retrieved the lasagna from the oven, popping the cheesy French bread under the broiler for a few minutes before taking it out. Killian set the table and opened a bottle of red wine I had on the counter, filling two goblets.

"I want to…but I feel oddly shy." I shook my head. "I can't tell you why, but it feels like the moment I open that book, I'm going to be dragged into something I won't be able to stop." I dished out a hearty serving of lasagna. "So, how did the clinic go today?"

Killian was a veterinarian who loved his work. The fact that he cared about animals so much endeared him to me even more. And even though he was a wolf shifter, he had a predilection for cats. He adored my pair, and they took advantage of that every time he was over.

"It was hard," he said, shrugging. "We had to put down a dog today. The poor thing leapt the fence and ran out in the road just as a truck came long. The driver tried to stop, but couldn't, and the dog…well…sometimes there's no fixing the damage."

I winced. "That's so hard. I'm sorry."

"Yeah, so was I. The owner tried—the fence was sturdy, but the dog was a good jumper and I guess he saw something he wanted to chase. These are the days that make it difficult. But I help when I can, that evens things out." He leaned back, taking a long sip of his wine. "So, remember a couple months ago when I told you my sister wanted to come visit once she was up and around?"

I froze, my fork in midair. "Yeah…?" Killian had also told me she wanted to meet me and spend some time getting to know me.

"She'll be here on Monday. I thought we could take her to dinner Monday night."

Even though I wanted to meet her, part of me was

afraid to. Shifter Packs and Prides tended to frown on intra-marriage—marriage between different species, so to speak—and some of them were even against intra-dating. But I couldn't tell Killian that. I didn't want him to think I was expecting a proposal, or that I didn't want to meet his family because I was a snob.

"Sure. What kind of food does she like?"

"Tally's got fairly simple tastes. She'll be happiest with a burger and fries." He grinned. "Made in the USA, so to speak."

"Then we can go to Lucky's. They make the best burgers in town." I forced a smile.

"You're upset," Killian said. "I can smell the shift."

Damn it. Shifters, especially wolf shifters, could smell the differences in body chemistry when their mates were upset, amorous, or afraid. Over the past couple months I had started to feel as though I was a living mood ring.

"No, not upset…" I paused.

"Then what? You can tell me," he said, frowning.

"I just… I know how some shifter families don't take to intra-species dating. I'm witchblood, you're a shifter."

"My parents and my sister aren't going to dislike you just because you're a witch and not a shifter. Trust me, please. I wouldn't ambush you like that—not if I thought Tally was going to be rude or anything of the sort." He sounded grumpy and looked grumpier. "Give me more credit than that. I'm not going to set you up for a fall."

I blushed. "I'm sorry, I never thought that. But you told me to tell you why I'm worried. Don't bite my head off when I do."

"I just… I thought you'd trust me more than that." Now he sounded hurt and that irritated me.

I let out a long sigh. "Don't twist my words. My worries have nothing to do with *you*. I'm concerned about how your relatives will feel about *me*. I have no fears that you're planning to ambush me or set me up for a fall. The fact is that I've got a history of bad interactions with in-laws, remember? Ellison's family hated the fact that I was witch-blood, so I'm already skittish about this whole *meet-the-family* thing. I'd feel the same way if you were human or a puma shifter or whatever else is hanging out there in the woods."

Killian shrugged, but I could tell he was still grumbly, and I felt my appetite vanish. We seldom argued, but now and then we had run across a definite difference of opinion. I had no desire for a volatile relationship, and he was usually pretty easygoing, but we were both stubborn and neither one of us was dewy fresh and new to the world of relationships.

"*Fine*," he said, toying with his lasagna. "You don't have to meet her."

"*Hold on there*. I *never* said I didn't want to meet your sister and you know it." I leaned back, crossing my arms. "All I said was that I was nervous. Don't you *dare* put words in my mouth."

"All right, all right. But you act—"

I leaned forward, almost accidentally sticking my boob in my lasagna. "Stop right there. I am acting like what I am: A woman nervous about meeting her boyfriend's family because she's worried they won't like her. Did it ever occur to you that the *reason* I'm nervous is because our relationship matters to me? Because *you* matter to me? Because I don't want to disappoint *them* when I meet them?" I glared at him.

Killian froze, then slowly deflated from the puffy stance he had adopted. "I didn't think of it like that."

"Well, I'd appreciate it if you would start looking at it from my perspective." I sighed and picked up my fork. "I just don't want to feel like a failure or like I've let you down."

"Love, I'm sorry," he said, wincing as he reached across the table for my hand. "I would *never* look at you like a failure. Even if my family didn't like you, I wouldn't blame you—unless you came out and called them names, or acted like an ass, and I know you too well to think you'd do that."

"Oh, for...eat your dinner," I said, gently disengaging my hand. "I'm too tired to argue over a misunderstanding." A thought occurred to me and I checked my phone. "Well, sure enough, we entered Mercury retrograde a couple days ago. Misunderstandings, miscommunications, don't sign contracts unless you read them carefully, watch appliances because they go on the fritz...all sorts of good stuff like that."

Killian nodded, shoveling a forkful of lasagna in his mouth. He was a Taurus, born on May 8, and stubborn as the bull that was his sign, but he also had a good head on his shoulders and he was reasonable when someone pointed out his flawed thinking.

"Ah, that explains it," he said. "My sister always has problems with misunderstandings and electronics during Mercury retrograde." He paused for a moment, then added, "I really am sorry, January. I didn't intentionally misunderstand what you said."

"I suppose I could have been a little clearer, too. I really am looking forward to meeting Tally. I just hope she likes me." I perked up again, feeling like we had just solved another minor roadblock on the path to what I hoped would be true love.

"She will," Killian said, perking up. "My sister and I have always tended to like each other's friends. Okay, so what are we doing tonight?"

"I'm taking a long bubble bath and then…" I paused. I loved having sex with Killian, but tonight I felt too tired, yet wired at the same time. I kept glancing over at Great-Grandma's book of shadows. "I kind of just want to read her diary, if you don't mind. It's been a long day."

Killian sighed, but it sounded like a sigh of relief. "Not a problem. I'm actually beat, too. Do you mind if I spend the night at my house? I want to do some laundry and I've got a bunch of email to answer and—"

I laughed, serving myself another helping of lasagna. "It's okay. We don't have to spend every moment together —*really*. I love our time together. I really like being with you. But we're not glued at the hip, and we don't have to do everything together. Life would be boring if all we wanted to do were the same things. I'm not a clingy woman."

He smiled then, broad and wide, and it made me rethink whether I was too tired for sex, but once again, I felt weary so I shook my head, beaming at him, and we finished our dinner in comfortable silence.

AFTER KILLIAN HELPED ME RINSE THE DISHES AND STACK them in the dishwasher, he again made certain the attic was closed up before he headed home. I watched him go, grateful that he had moved in next door. I not only enjoyed dating him, but I liked having him for a friend.

I shrugged into a jacket and headed out to my backyard. As usual, the Mystic Wood was lit up like a tree on fire—or a hundred trees on fire. The golden-green aura of the magical woodland was brilliant tonight. Not everyone could see it, but most of us who were witchblood could.

I slowly crossed the lawn to where I was standing about twenty yards from the tree line. I scanned the border where my property met the forest, looking for anything that might be lurking in the shadows. There was some sort of imp in there—her name was Rebecca, or rather, that's the name she had given me when I was a child and she tried to lure me away from my mother. I had seen her once since I had been back in Moonshadow Bay, but I had promised that if she left me alone, I'd leave her alone. I didn't like that she was in the wood, but I had the feeling I could do more damage to her at this point than she could to me.

I stared up at the tops of the trees. They were budding out, the green tips swelling. Soon they'd burgeon out into leaves, and the conifers would be interspersed with the spring green of birch and alder and cottonwood leaves. My yard was fenced, half an acre that was surrounded by trees on both sides and the Mystic Wood at the back. The trees that bordered the fencing on either side of the house and yard included two massive cedar trees and a number of fir, one sequoia that jutted its way far into the sky, and a weeping sequoia that reminded me of some lurching long-haired creature from out of an enchanted fairytale. I also had a number of rowan and lilac trees, a holly tree, and several maple trees. They, too, were budding, and I looked forward to the heady scent of lilacs in two or three months.

All in all, the yard was beautiful and the house well-kept, and the only thing that kept me from truly loving it was that I now owned it, which meant my parents were dead. But I wasn't about to sell it to some stranger who might cut down my mother's row of hydrangeas that lined the right side of the house, or who might sell to a developer who would parcel it out into tiny lots with mega-mansions on it. We were lucky in Moonshadow Bay, because there were some strict ordinances in place to ensure that developers wouldn't tear the town to pieces in search of the holy grail filled with dollars. So throughout the years, the town's quirky charm remained intact.

As I stood by the edge of the wood, I felt a gentle pulse from the pentacle I wore around my neck. It had a faceted obsidian cabochon in the center, and it had belonged to my mother. I wore it because it felt right, and because Esmara had told me to. I reached up and closed my hand around it, shutting my eyes, feeling the chill breeze sweep over me. I could smell the bay on the wind—the scent of seaweed and salt, of brine and decay. Even here, the incoming tides brought the smell of the Salish Sea inland, and seagulls flew overhead, a constant in the town, singing their melancholy songs.

I crouched, pressing my hands to the ground, feeling the slow beat of the earth through my fingers. I had recently found out that my aunt had pledged me to Druantia, an earth goddess, when I was little. She had done so in order to protect me from the shadow man who tried to steal away my life while I was in her care. In a recent meditation, Druantia had offered me the chance to break that pledge if I wanted, but I let it stand. I wasn't sure what being pledged to her meant, but the connection felt right. She was part of the earth's heartbeat, and through her, I felt linked to the natural world around me.

I listened to the astral breeze as the wind ruffled my hair. I had swept it back into a long ponytail, but several strands had escaped and were tickling my face and my neck.

And then, I heard it—what I had been waiting for. The soft chatter of the crocus, the low tones of trees talking together as they woke from their slumber, and the murmur of those who watched during the winter— tall sentinels who watched over the woodland. The swish of a huckleberry bush caught my attention, and I knew that a fox had run through the boughs. And there, barely within the tree line, the soft slithering of a garden snake—early in the year, but slowly waking to summer. There was a world of activity going on around me, a world that most people never paid attention to or even noticed.

I narrowed my focus, tuning into the massive entity that made up the heart of the Mystic Wood. It was crafty and devious, beautiful and bewitching, enchanting and dangerous, and yet…there was nothing evil about the woodland. But still, the wood was a deadly place for the unwary.

We're waiting…

I froze, watching, but still nothing moved, and finally I backed away until I was halfway up the lawn. Then I turned and jogged toward the house. Whoever had been talking to me hadn't been Esmara, that much I knew. And it hadn't been Druantia. No, whoever had whispered those words lived deep inside the forest and right now, I didn't want to meet them.

Back inside, I locked the door and leaned back against it, my stomach in knots. I reached for the light switch and turned the kitchen lights fully up. The energy had spooked me more than I had expected it to. As I calmed down, I started to move away from the door when a loud thump against it sent me spinning around. As I watched, the handle of the door turned, but the door was locked. It jiggled once more as I stared at it, then I heard something sliding across the porch. I was considering turning on the porch light and looking outside, but the thought of what might happen stopped me.

I waited for a moment, then—as the sounds vanished —I cautiously edged up to the door window and peeked out. In the darkness, there was nothing that I could see. I bit my lip and flipped on the porch light, but all I could see was a trail of mud on the porch floor. It wasn't even muddy footprints, just a slick of mud from the screen door to the back door. I waited for a couple minutes and then shut off the porch light again, double-checking the lock.

What was that? I asked, hoping Esmara could hear me.

I'm not certain, but you've attracted the attention of the forest. I don't sense danger...per se...or rather—evil. Everything in the Mystic Wood can be dangerous.

Am I safe?

Are we ever safe? But yes, child, you're as safe as you can be, for living on the edge of a magical wood.

With that thought, I considered reading some of my great-grandmother's journal before bed, but I was suddenly so tired that even the thought of it seemed overwhelming. I checked the doors downstairs, made sure the range and oven were off, and slowly trudged up the stairs to take a shower with Xi and Klaus right outside. After a long soak under the steaming water, I curled up in bed, turned on the TV, and with both kittens snuggled against me, I fell asleep to reruns of *Frasier*.

SUNDAY DAWNED CLEAR AND COOL. FOR WESTERN Washington, "clear" meant partially cloudy but with sun peeking through. We had very few cloud-free days per year—about sixty of them, from what I had read. For the most part, a "clear day" meant that we saw several sunbreaks throughout the day.

I had slept restlessly, with vague dreams of creatures hiding in the dark, waiting for me as I wandered through a dark woodland. Relieved to be awake, I dressed in capri pants and a pinup top with ruched sides and a sweetheart neckline. At a size 14 going on 16, I had an hourglass figure and plenty of padding. I liked my curves, though, and finally I was free from toxic people in my life trying to shame me for my size.

I was also five-nine, tall for most women, but I didn't give a damn—I wore high heels whenever I wanted to. My hair was long and—currently red—it cascaded down my back in waves. Ari had dyed it burgundy with a gloss of violet for my birthday, and I loved it so much I decided to keep the color for a while. The color set off my eyes, which were hazel.

I slipped on a pair of ballerina flats and headed downstairs, only to find that somehow Xi and Klaus had managed to open the cupboard where I kept the dry cat food, and they had chewed through the bag. Kibble was scattered all over the kitchen, the bag was slumped over like a soldier who had fought valiantly to the end, and both kittens stared at me with wide, innocent eyes.

"Oh, don't give me that look," I said. "I know you did it."

Xi squeaked and grabbed another kibble, chewing on it. Klaus sat down, staring at the food like he wanted to dive in again but wasn't sure whether I was going to scold him. I tried not to laugh as I found the dustpan and whiskbroom and swept up the mess. Then I filled their dishes and opened a can of gooshy food for them, and before they could dive in, I scooped them up for a cuddle and a kiss on the head. Klaus, eyeing the food, wriggled out of my arms and lightly jumped down to the floor.

But Xi looked into my eyes and I fell into her gaze, my heart melting. She was growing into my familiar, and while I loved animals, I hadn't realized just how strong of a bond could form, or how quickly it could form. While Klaus wore his emotions on his paw, Xi I could feel in the core of my being.

"Yeah, you're a little spitfire, you are," I whispered as she gently batted my nose. "Go eat, you little goober."

I fixed myself a mocha and, glancing in the fridge, decided to have a sandwich for breakfast. I slapped together French bread, turkey breast, lettuce, tomato, and butter, and carried it over to the table where I sat down and took a bite of the sandwich. Then, like someone who had put off paying the bills too long, I gingerly reached for Colleen's book of shadows. Taking a deep breath, I dove in, turning back the hands of time as I began to explore the past.

Colleen's Book of Shadows
Entry: May 7, 1915

The ley lines are strong in this land, they cross over the town in a number of positions and they make everyone's magic so much more powerful. The forest itself is alive, and filled with dreadful and wondrous creatures. We never expected, when we founded Moonshadow Bay, for the town to come alive so quickly.

The natives won't come here—they warned us off. They're friendly to us, unlike a number of the settlers around here, because we respect them and their customs. Johnny Salmon-Diver made a special trip here to talk to Brian and me, since we were the ones who first established Moonshadow Bay.

While he acknowledged our magic might be able to keep some of the chaos out, he warned that this particular area of the bay is considered off limits to the Nooksack tribe because it belongs to the "others." We asked if there was a way we could cleanse the land and he said no—the "old ones" have lived here so long that they've left an indelible marker on the area. When we asked him to clarify who he was talking about, he refused to speak more of them, saying only that it attracted their attention when their names were used or people discussed them.

Johnny said that he wouldn't be able to come

again because his tribe didn't want him to bring home any attachments—spirits are known to do that, of course. And apparently, around here, not only do spirits of the dead frequent the area, but other entities. When I asked him to what he was referring, Johnny would only say that here, the "others" were dangerous and bewitching, and to avoid the woods at night, and never let children near the Mystic Wood unattended.

I sat back, staring at the passage. So, even *before* the town had been founded, the Native Americans had known about the woodland. I pushed back the book, thinking. Maybe it wasn't chance that had drawn my great-grandparents to Moonshadow Bay. Maybe it was fate.

I believed in fate, to a degree. I didn't believe everything was preordained—predestination didn't allow for free will and above all, I believed that we could change the outcome of almost any situation. Oh, everyone died, and if we didn't pay our taxes we'd eventually end up in jail, but other than that—there was usually a choice.

While I did believe certain things were slated to happen and that we were sometimes born to a path in life, that didn't mean that every step, every movement, every choice was already set before us. I didn't believe in perfection, and life wouldn't be a challenge if we had no choices. If people didn't believe they had some sort of control over the outcome of their lives, it would strip away the desire to strive and succeed.

I shrugged, and glanced over the next few entries.

There were several recipes for spells and rituals to be done by moonlight, or during the afternoon—even one to do at seven A.M. on a Saturday morning to invoke clarity. Great-Grandma Colleen had been detailed when it came to her magic. I randomly flipped to another passage. By then, my great-grandparents had three children, and Moonshadow Bay had been in existence twelve years.

Colleen's Book of Shadows
Entry: December 15, 1918

Well, life moves along. I'm exhausted. Who knew how tiring raising children can be? I love them, and I love my family, but the wee ones are enough to tax the strongest of hearts and souls, and with a babe still in diapers, and a five-year-old and a three-year-old, I'm run ragged. Brian suggested I find a nursemaid, and so I plan on it. I'll put an advert in the *Moonshadow Bay Monitor* tomorrow.

The town may be small, but there are plenty of young women looking for work, especially among the shifter clans. They betroth their girls young, so there's no need for the women to spend time on husband-finding. And shifters are long-lived, so there are several candidates among the wolf-shifter Packs who are looking for something to occupy their time until they get married.

I went into the Mystic Wood the other day and much to my chagrin, I discovered a turnstone. I hadn't expected to find such a thing here—I thought it was native to my beloved England. Or Ireland, rather—given I'm an Irish lass by blood. I do miss my childhood home, but I even miss England. But Brian wanted to emigrate and true enough, our fortunes have grown multi-fold since we moved here. He has founded his legal practice and is the leading barrister in the town. *Lawyer*, they call it here. Anyway, I digress.

So yes, I found a turnstone, and that worries me. That means the Woodlings have found their way across the ocean. Or perhaps they've always been here? Per chance they're found worldwide, by differing names? But I know for sure they are settled in the Mystic Wood, and who knows how many they have swept away?

I plan on bringing this up at the next Witches' Council, but I'm sure that Rowan Firesong will try to waylay my worries and act as though nothing is the matter. I'm not sure why she seems to dislike me. She definitely does her best to ingratiate herself with Brian. I'm grateful I trust him, but she *is* pretty and sometimes...I wonder. I just have to hope he ignores her charms and still carries his torch for me, and that nothing will come of my concerns...

I shut the book and pushed it aside, taking care so that it was well away from the remains of my breakfast. What on earth was a *turnstone*? And why did my great-grand-mother think it might only exist back in her homeland?

Esmara, are you there?

No answer. I tried again and still no answer. Apparently, the Ladies were out lunching on the spiritual plane. I debated on whether to continue reading but then I remembered I had laundry to do and the house to clean, and Ari was coming over in the early afternoon. She wanted to introduce me to a friend of hers who was in from out of town, whom she thought I'd like to meet.

I finished my breakfast and downed the rest of my mocha and then hustled my ass upstairs to put a load of clothes in the laundry. I added detergent, set the controls, and then changed the sheets. As soon as I was done with that, I swept and mopped my bedroom, cleaned the bathroom, and then moved on to downstairs, where I swept like a whirlwind through the house. Luckily, I was a fairly neat person, and I tended to clean up after myself as I went.

I loaded the dishwasher with the breakfast dishes and since I hadn't run it after dinner the previous evening, I set it to cycle. I kept glancing back at the table, at Colleen's book of shadows. What else would I learn about my great-grandmother's life? I now knew that she had been jealous of Rowan Firesong, and that was something that I'd have to figure out how to approach Rowan about. If I talked to her about it at all.

After I finished mopping the kitchen, I tidied the living room and then I was done. Cleaning had taken me an hour, tops, and now it was time to change the laundry out and put another load in.

"I'd love to have a maid," I muttered.

No, you wouldn't. You'd resent someone in your space, around your things. Which is why your mother never hired help.

I jumped. Sometimes the Ladies were downright sneaky. *You startled me! Esmara, I found Colleen's book of shadows.*

Good. Read it all the way through. It will take some time, but there are so many things in there you can use to help you hone your magic.

She was jealous of Rowan.

Well, yes, we know that now, but my sisters and I never realized it then.

Is Colleen with the Ladies? I don't think I've ever heard you mention her.

You've barely heard me mention anything, given I only appeared a few months ago to guide you. But no, Colleen...to be honest, we're not sure what happened to her. Your mother, however, has joined the Ladies. And you...well...you have many things to do in Moonshadow Bay. So much more before you.

I paused, wanting to ask her what, but I knew she wouldn't tell me. *Is there anything in particular I should be doing now?*

Remember to contact the Aseer and set up an appointment. You will have to talk to her about Rowan being your grand-mother, so don't overlook that. And with that, she fell silent.

That's right—I almost forgot. I sighed, setting a reminder on my phone to call the Aseer.

I washed my hands and was about to settle down with Colleen's book of shadows again when the doorbell rang. I opened the door to find Ari there, with a woman who was curvier and shorter than me. She was dressed in a waist-cinching 1950s swing dress, a cropped jacket, kitten heels, and a pair of red-framed, horn-rimmed glasses. Her hair was as coppery as Ari's and she had a winsome smile. But her gaze was sharp, and I had the feeling she observed in detail everything that went on around her.

"Hey, come on in." I motioned them into the living room.

Ari led her friend into the living room before turning to introduce us. "January, this is Peggin Sanderson. She lives in Whisper Hollow, out on the peninsula. Peggin, this is my bestie, January Jaxson."

As I reached out to shake Peggin's hand, a spark hit me hard, and I knew right then I was talking to someone with a very deep magical, very shadowed energy behind her.

CHAPTER THREE

*P*eggin took my hand, her eyes widening and I could tell she felt the crackle of magic, too. "Oh man, you're strong in the force," she said with a giggle. "Nice to meet you."

"Good to meet you, too," I said. "Whisper Hollow…" I ran the name around on my tongue. It sounded familiar but I couldn't quite place it. "I don't think I've been there."

"It's over on the shores of Crescent Lake," she said. "Unless you were called, or unless you dropped in and the town wanted you to forget you had, you probably haven't been there. Whisper Hollow, like Moonshadow Bay, attracts a certain type of resident."

By the way she said it, I knew immediately what she meant. Towns like Moonshadow Bay and Whisper Hollow were near to invisible for people who weren't supposed to be there. The magical towns blended into the background, and signs announcing their presence on the highways and freeways went unseen by those not meant to traverse their streets.

I nodded. "Well, sit down, both of you. Would you rather sit in the kitchen? I can make us mochas or lattes or whatever you like. Have you had lunch yet?"

"We were actually thinking of taking you out to lunch," Ari said.

"All right. Why don't we go to the Spit & Whistle Pub? When do you want to go?" I glanced at the clock.

"We can head out now. Later, I was thinking we could take a walk out into the Mystic Wood and give Peggin a feel for the area."

I laughed. "Oh, I'm sure she'll like *that*. The Mystic Wood is dangerous, Peggin. A lot of creatures live there who don't fancy strangers."

She grinned. "You've obviously never been to Whisper Hollow."

"Peggin's right, Whisper Hollow is more dangerous than Moonshadow Bay," Ari said to me. "Before you moved back, Meagan and I began going over to the peninsula for day trips. We'd take the ferry over to Port Townsend and drive along the highway, skirting the edge of the peninsula. One day, we saw the sign for Whisper Hollow and stopped in. We met Peggin at the farmers market. We asked her about the town and the three of us just hit it off."

While the most I'd ever heard of Whisper Hollow was in a passing comment or two, now, with Ari talking about it, the aura of the town seemed to surround Peggin. I shivered.

She comes from the land of the dead, Esmara whispered.
What do you mean? She's dead?
No, but she is steeped in the energy of the grave—Whisper Hollow is a crossing place, riddled with ley lines just like

Moonshadow Bay, only it sits closer to the Veil. And Peggin has been touched by the energy of the Veil—I can see it in her aura.

I said nothing, but asked, "How long will you be in Moonshadow Bay?"

"For a few days, then I'll head home on Thursday. I was going to stop into Seattle this trip, but it's so pretty here that I think I'll postpone that and spend the time here instead." She paused, then added, "January, you remind me of my best friend. She's…" She stopped as her stomach rumbled. Laughing, she said, "Why don't we go for lunch? I'm famished."

"My car or yours?" I asked Ari. I had just bought a brand-new Ocelot, a sleek, compact SUV. I actually missed Cookie, my old car, but she had outlived her days.

Ari shrugged. "Mine—it's easier that way."

I glanced at Peggin's kitten heels. "When we *do* go out into the woods, you'd better change shoes. It's pretty muddy out there."

She laughed. "You'd be surprised where I can wear these babies. But I brought a pair of boots with me. They're at Ari's."

Now curious about Whisper Hollow and Peggin's life, I gathered my purse, slid into a jacket, and followed them out to Ari's car.

Peggin pointed to my capri pants. "Those are cute. Where did you get them?"

"I ordered them from Swept, a website with a lot of really cute clothes for those of us who aren't Ari's size and who want something different than what you find in the stores." I grinned at her. Peggin was probably close to a size 14, though she was shorter than I was and had a

Marilyn Monroe hourglass figure with bigger hips and boobs.

"I'll have to look for them," she said.

THE SPIT & WHISTLE WAS FULL UP, SO WE OPTED FOR Lucky's Diner rather than waiting. The diner had a retro feel to it, and the best diner food around. As we sat in a booth next to one of the large windows, I went over to the jukebox. It was actually digital, but it was made to look like one of the old ones. I popped in a quarter and selected a song by Outasight—a boppy number called "Bounce."

When the waitress came, I ordered mac 'n cheese and fried chicken, Peggin ordered a hamburger and fries, and Ari ordered a bowl of chowder. We all succumbed to the lure of milkshakes and filled the time until our food arrived with chatter. The more I talked to her, the more I liked Peggin, even though Esmara's comment stuck in my brain.

We were almost done with lunch when my phone rang. I didn't recognize the number, so stepped away from the booth to answer. "Hello?"

"Is this the Magical Web?" a woman asked.

The Magical Web was a business Ari and I were running on the side. While she had a full-time hair salon business, and I worked for Conjure Ink, a paranormal investigations agency, we had decided to branch out and take on occasional cases that were too small for Conjure Ink but too big for the clients to handle on their own.

"Yes, this is. January Jaxson speaking. How may I help you?"

"My name is Tabitha Sweet, and I'm… I need help. I've talked to the police and they won't do anything." She sounded frantic.

"What's wrong? Are you in danger?" Ari and I had decided that was the first thing we would ask, because psychics occasionally received calls from someone who was under actual physical duress.

"I don't know…it's about my baby."

"If you need medical assistance—"

"No, it's not like that. I don't know how to explain it. I've talked to my doctor, and I've talked to the cops, and none of them can do anything. But I know that she's not my child. Someone stole my baby and put this…creature…in her place. Can you help me?"

I debated. There was a fine line, at times, between someone who was being affected by the paranormal and someone who needed psychological help. And that line wasn't always easy to spot. "All right, calm down. When would you like to meet?"

"Can you come over this afternoon? I know I sound crazy, but I'm not, I assure you."

I muted her and turned to Ari. "We may have a case. Either that or we'd better have a good therapist's number ready. She wants to meet with us this afternoon. Can you make it?"

Ari glanced at Peggin. "Will you be okay on your own for an hour or so?"

Peggin snorted. "*No*, I'm too needy for that. *Of course* I'll be fine. I'll walk around town, do some shopping, and if your appointment runs long, I can take in a movie."

"It probably won't take more than an hour," I said, "but in that case, we'll head over there after we finish lunch. Then Ari can drop me off at home, and pick you up."

"If you get tired, just take a cab home," Ari said. "You have the address and I'll give you a key."

"Actually," Peggin said, "if you drop me off at your house before your appointment, I can take my own car downtown and then maybe drive around the bay for a bit."

I told Tabitha we'd be there in an hour or so. After that, we lingered over our lunch, which Ari insisted on paying for, then drove back to Ari's house where we dropped off Peggin. She waved, looking quite happy to meander on her own for a while.

As we headed for Tabitha's house, I filled Ari in on what the client had told me. "I'm not sure what's going on," I said, "but she sounded absolutely frantic."

"I can think of several potential causes, the most notable one that she might need a therapist," Ari said. "But maybe something's clouding her sight? Maybe the baby's picked up an attachment. It's rare for someone so young, but it's not unheard of."

"Yeah. Whatever the case turns out to be, we need to make certain that nothing we do will hurt the child, and that she's not so distraught that *she* would try to hurt the girl. If we have any doubts, we contact Millie and have her call Child Protective Services. Agreed?"

"Agreed," Ari said.

We stopped at my house to pick up my bag of magical supplies, then drove to the other side of town where Tabitha Sweet lived. When Tabitha met us at the door, I immediately pegged her as human. She seemed to have some psychic abilities, but she wasn't witchblood.

"Thank you for coming," she said, letting us in. "I was afraid you wouldn't."

"What seems to be the problem?" I asked as she led us into the bungalow. It was tidy—neat as a pin, actually—and everything felt very cozy. However, as I searched for any protective magic or wards, I could sense nothing. The house was wide open and vulnerable. "You have no magical protection on your house at all, do you?"

She shrugged. "I never thought I'd need it. I'm not witchblood, and neither is my daughter."

"How old is she?"

"She's barely a year old. She just turned a year last week. But…" She paused, looking thoroughly miserable.

"What's wrong? Why don't you start at the beginning?" Ari said. "May we sit down?"

"Oh, where are my manners?" Her hand flew to her mouth and she looked miserable. "I'm so sorry. Come in, please, and have a seat. Would you like something to drink?"

"We just had lunch, thank you, so we're fine." As I sat down on the leather sofa in the living room, I looked around. The room was shabby chic, but it looked deliberately decorated, not like she had tried to spruce it up on a thrift-store budget.

"My name is Tabitha, but you know that."

"Who lives here with you?" Ari said. "Besides your daughter? And what is her name?"

"Zoey and I live here alone. Her father—my ex-boyfriend—moved out seven months ago. We broke up. He pays his child support, but he wasn't ready to be a father. He wants nothing to do with either of us. I have sole custody. He left me his medical records so if we ever need information regarding her medical heritage, we have it, but he said he doesn't want to hear from her. *Ever.*" She hung her head. "I don't know what I'll tell her as she grows up."

"All right, so the father is out of the picture. You and Zoey live here alone?"

She nodded. "Now. I had a live-in nanny, but she left two weeks ago. I think she stole Zoey."

I glanced at Ari, raising my eyebrows just the slightest bit. "Why do you say that?"

"Because the baby in that room isn't my baby. I know. *Mothers know*, damn it!" Tabitha threw up her hands, bursting into tears. "The cops think I'm off my rocker, and so does my doctor. I took Zoey in to his office the other day, demanding he test her blood. He did. He said that there's no doubt it's Zoey. He told me that I'm under a lot of stress and to get some rest. But I know my baby, and the creature in that crib is *not my Zoey*."

"And you think the nanny left…a *replacement*? Or do you think that the baby's possessed?"

"Either…both…I don't know." Tabitha nodded, her tears staining her face. "She looks like Zoey and sounds like Zoey, and apparently has the same blood type, but I know my baby, and that thing isn't Zoey."

"Can we meet her?" I said.

Tabitha nodded. "I'll get her—"

"Why don't you just take us into her room?" Ari interjected.

Tabitha led us into the nursery. At first glance, everything seemed normal. There were piles of toys around the room, though tidy piles, and a rocking chair painted white, with the walls a pale blush pink. The crib was over in the corner, away from the window, and inside was a beautiful little girl. I had little to no maternal drive—except when it came to animals—but she was cute enough and when we entered the room, she stood and reached out for Tabitha, who just stared at her.

Ari hoisted the baby into her arms, propping her against one hip. "Well, hello there." She gave Tabitha a long look, then said, "If you'd leave us alone for a few minutes?"

Tabitha nodded and, without a single look back at the baby, left the room, shutting the door behind her. Ari let out a sigh and sat down in the rocking chair. I sat on the ottoman next to her.

"So, what the hell is going on? Should we report her to CPS?"

"The baby looks well fed. I don't think she's skimping on care for the child, except in the emotional arena. Did you see that look Tabitha shot her?" Ari shook her head. "All right, let's take a look at you," she said to Zoey.

We looked at the baby, who was wearing a onesie. I took the baby's onesie off and we checked her for any noticeable marks, but there were none. In fact, her skin looked incredibly smooth. As far as I knew all babies had smooth skin, but there was something different about Zoey. I just couldn't pinpoint what was it was.

"She looks fine, and the doctor's report said she's healthy. But…now that we're alone with her, I do feel something odd. It's like…" I paused, trying to pinpoint my feeling. "Can you feel anything?"

Ari nodded. "Yeah, though I can't pin it down."

At that moment, Zoey looked at me, and I caught something in her eyes—a sneakiness of sorts. There was something slightly feral about her, and it concerned me. "I'm not sure what's going on, but I think Tabitha is right. Now whether this is actually her daughter Zoey, I don't know. But there's something...*odd* about the child. She unsettles me," I said, staring back at the baby. "She seems so much...older."

"Older, yes. And she's listening to us," Ari said, very slowly holding the baby away from her. "I'm putting her back in the crib."

She settled the child back in the crib and stepped away. I was watching Zoey's expression and instead of the bland baby stare, once again a feral light entered the baby's eyes. The moment she caught me looking at her, it vanished and she gurgled and waved her hands toward Ari.

I had a strong feeling that I shouldn't bring out my magical gear in front of the baby. "Ari, let's step into the hallway. Bye, Zoey!" I waved to the child, who was sitting in the crib. Without missing a beat, she waved back, and not in that frantic hand-flailing way a lot of babies had.

I shut the door behind me. "I'd rather not discuss this here. I want to take the case, and tell the mother we're not sure what's going on, but we'll look into it. That will hopefully prevent her from doing anything she can't take back."

Ari nodded. "Good idea."

We returned to the living room, where Tabitha was waiting, an anxious look on her face.

"We're not sure what's going on. I need to bring a couple pieces of equipment next time I come, so if you could, just go about things as if they're normal. I don't recommend telling anybody else what you suspect. *If*

Zoey isn't your child, we don't want to tip off whoever exchanged her. All right?" I wanted to ensure that Tabitha didn't talk her way right into a psych ward, not until we could suss out whatever energy was hovering around that child.

Tabitha nodded, her expression serious. "Then you don't think I'm crazy?"

"No, not at all," I said. Even if she was having a breakdown, there was something going on, and whatever it was could easily have an impact on Tabitha's mental state. A number of people in mental hospitals were victims of psychic attacks or walk-ins, or they were psychics themselves who hadn't realized they had power and it was overwhelming them.

We left, after making her promise to take care of Zoey like she were her own child.

Once we were back in the car, Ari sat back, shaking her head. "What did you see in there? I know you picked up on something. I felt some creepy stuff, too, but I'm not sure what it was."

"When you put Zoey back in her crib, she gave me the creepiest stare. Tabitha's right, that's not your run-of-the-mill baby. Whether it's actually Zoey and Zoey is possessed, or something that we don't know about, I'm not sure. But something's up with the kid. I want to borrow some equipment from work, if Tad will let me, and set up a surveillance in the nursery." I couldn't shake the feeling that we were dealing with some sort of possession, but I didn't want to bias myself in advance. Objectivity was absolutely necessary when working in the psychic sphere.

"Whatever the case, there's something odd there." Ari

shook her head. "I have a strange feeling about this case. Did you ask for a retainer when I wasn't paying attention?"

I shook my head. "I will, but right now I want to talk to Tad first, and see if I can borrow or rent a surveillance camera from Conjure Ink." I paused for a moment. Then, because we hadn't had time before, I said, "Esmara told me something about your friend Peggin."

"What?" Ari asked.

"She said that Peggin 'comes from the land of the dead.' That she carries the energy of the grave with her, and that Whisper Hollow is a 'crossing place'…riddled with ley lines, like Moonshadow Bay."

Ari nodded. "Yeah, well, Peggin's best friend is a spirit shaman. So that would make sense."

I was taken aback. "Peggin's best friend is a *spirit shaman*? Spirit shamans drive the dead back across the Veil when they aren't supposed to return." I shivered. "I had no idea there were any in Washington. But it makes sense. There are towns around the peninsula that are so close to the Veil that the dead find it an easy place to cross back over."

Part of me wanted to go over to Whisper Hollow and meet Peggin's friend. I was always fascinated when I ran into other forms of witches and seers, but I decided to wait and see if it happened naturally. I didn't want to invite unnecessary chaos into my life, and from every-thing I understood, spirit shamans were steeped in chaotic energy, though unlike chaos magicians, they didn't *try* to summon it.

"All right, let's focus on Tabitha and Zoey. We need to figure out whether the baby's possessed or…" I paused, thinking. "Or is Tabitha off her rocker? I tend to believe the former, but if Tabitha does need help, we'll have to contact Child Protective Services."

With that thought in mind, Ari drove us back to my place. "What do you think about taking a walk in the woods this evening? I can bring Peggin over tonight."

I nodded. "Sounds good. Do you mind if I invite Killian to go with us? I'm not certain how safe I feel to go tramping around the Mystic Wood without him with us."

"That's fine. Bring the wolf." Ari laughed. "I'm so glad you found him. You've been so happy, and so much more...yourself...than you *ever* were when you were with Ellison."

"Killian gives me space to be myself. Say, Peggin won't weird out at being around a shifter, will she?" Even though Killian looked plenty human, his alt-form had a definite presence.

"She's used to it. The spirit shaman's boyfriend is a wolf shifter, too," Ari said, dropping me off. "I'll be back with Peggin around seven P.M., if that's okay. After dinner."

"See you then!" I waved. I was inserting my key in the lock when Esmara startled me.

Someday you'll meet the spirit shaman, she said. *And when that day comes, you'll have things to learn from each other. And you'll understand what it's like to walk with the dead surrounding you.*

On that cheery note, I unlocked the door, relieved to be home.

CHAPTER FOUR

*J*t was nearly four o'clock. I called Killian, but he was still at the clinic and told me he'd be home around six. "That's fine," I said. "Come over as soon as you can for dinner. Ari wants to take a friend of hers out into the Mystic Wood, so I was hoping you'd come along."

"You think that's wise?" he asked.

"Hey, this woman can handle it—that I'm pretty sure of. So, dress for the weather."

"Okay. I'm glad I don't have clinic hours tonight, to be honest. I'm tired." He made kissing noises before hanging up.

Killian was working about seventy hours a week. Establishing a new business usually meant long hours for the first year, and although he had the experience, he still had to establish clientele here and convince them he would handle their beloved pets with care and kindness.

I didn't mind the long hours, because I often worked

late, too. Although I didn't usually work on weekends, I still had plenty of chores and activities to occupy my time.

After hanging my coat on the hall pegs, I went upstairs to move the last load of laundry over to the dryer. I hung up the wet clothes that couldn't go through a drying cycle, then returned to the kitchen where I poked around the fridge, trying to decide what to make for dinner.

Lunch had been filling, so I decided to fix something a little lighter. I decided to make grilled cheese sandwiches and tomato soup. I set out all the ingredients and pans I would need, set the table, and then stopped to play with Xi and Klaus for a bit. They bounced around, climbing on my lap when I sat down and turned on the TV.

I had gotten rid of my landline and cable, opting for a streaming service for my TV. I flipped through the shows, settling for *The Greatest Cake Competition*. I had no aspirations to become the next big baker, but I did love watching the contestants build their fantastical creations. They were competing in a show for spring cakes, and as I expected, bunnies and chicks abounded.

Twenty minutes later, the kittens were sleeping and I turned off the TV, thinking about Zoey. I gave my boss, Tad Gelphart, a call. "Hey, Tad, what are you doing?"

"You really want to know?" he asked, sounding wrung out.

"Only if it's G or PG rated, thank you."

"I just finished a game of handball at the gym. I did *not* win. I didn't even come close. I can run a seven-minute mile, but I don't have the best coordination," he grumped.

"Well, at least you got some exercise in. That's better than I did. Listen, I was wondering…"

"That's dangerous," he said, laughing. "I'm beginning to

believe that when you start thinking, things start to happen."

"Oh, *shuddup*, dude," I said, but I laughed along with him. "Do you mind if Ari and I borrow a couple pieces of equipment from Conjure Ink? We have a case that frankly…well, I'm not sure what to think." I sighed, once again feeling torn between whether I thought Tabitha was a little off her rocker, or paranoid with a good reason.

Tad sobered. "What's up?"

"Our client believes that someone stole her baby and replaced the girl with an exact replica. At first I thought it might be postpartum depression that's led into a worse disorder, but after meeting the child…there *is* something odd about her, Tad. I'm confused, to be honest. I don't know what to think."

"What do you mean, *odd*?"

I sighed. "I can't give you an exact reason but…the baby scares me a little. She's only supposed to be a year old, but there's an alertness to her that speaks to her being much, much older. And she's crafty. I normally wouldn't say that about a baby, but damn, she made me nervous. Ari, too. There was a look the baby gave me that I have to say felt threatening."

"Could have it been the power of suggestion from the mother?"

"I suppose anything's possible. When I first heard Tabitha's story, I thought she might be off a bit, until I met the child. There's something wrong, Tad. I'm not sure if the baby's possessed or what, but there's a darkness around her." I paused, then asked, "Have you ever heard of a replacement? I was thinking maybe a walk-in?"

Walk-ins were when a spirit walked into a body and

took control. It was similar to possession, but more often than not, the spirit who had inhabited that body left, leaving the body alive but without a consciousness, and the walk-in could drive the body like we drove a car. It happened more when people fell into a coma, or went into extreme trauma.

"What about a changeling?" Tad asked. "That used to be a common thing in areas where the Fae live. And I know that some Fae inhabit the Mystic Wood."

*Fae...*I hadn't even though about *them*. Stories about changelings came flooding back.

"That would track. I kind of thought that changelings were like the boogeyman—stories to frighten kids into being good."

"Maybe some stories were used for that, but I'm pretty sure the legend of the changelings is actually a real… thing, so to speak. What equipment did you want to borrow?"

"A security camera, for one thing. Maybe one of the FLIRs, and an EMF device?" We had all the latest ghost-hunting equipment at the office, but it proved handy for other creatures too.

"Sign it out, and as long as you pay for it if it breaks, we're good. When do you want to pick it up?"

"Tomorrow. I have plans this evening. Thanks." I hung up and turned back to the kittens. "Well, you two, shall we start dinner?" With both fluffy butts following me, I returned to the kitchen and began fixing the soup and sandwiches.

KILLIAN ARRIVED WITH ROSES AND A KISS. "I KNOW YOU'RE good with me working late so often, but these are just a thank-you for understanding."

"Of course I understand. You think I don't work late every now and then? It's okay." I took the flowers and put them in a vase, kissing him. "Thank you, these are beautiful. Dinner's ready, so help me carry food to the table?"

As I stacked the grilled cheese sandwiches on a plate, then ladled out soup mugs of the tomato soup, Killian carried them to the table. He glanced at my great-grandma's book of shadows.

"Have you started reading it yet?"

I nodded. "Yeah. I found out that Colleen was jealous of Rowan Firesong. It's weird to think that my grandmother was alive when my great-grandfather was. I mean, I know I'll be long-lived too, but…"

"I was alive then," Killian said, his voice soft.

I arched my eyebrows. "I know. The age difference doesn't bother me, honest." Killian was 120 years old. He had been born in 1900. "How old is your sister? Your brother and your parents?"

"Tally's younger than I am. She was born in 1930. Darryn was born in 1950. So I'm the oldest. My parents are about 160. They were both born in 1861, and they married in 1888." He bit into his sandwich, the cheese oozing out.

I thought for a moment, then asked, "Shifters have a long period of fertility, don't they?"

He nodded. "Our women—at least with wolf shifters—can get pregnant well toward 100."

"What did you do before you became a veterinarian?"

He laughed. "I've always been one. Although the term

'veterinarian' has only been around since about the 1600s, animal doctors have abounded since the days of ancient Egypt and before that. I knew when I was young that I wanted to treat animals, so I attended school for it back in 1920. I've kept up with all the changes throughout all the years, and of course, being a shifter, I found that it helps that I could talk to wolves and dogs. Cats were harder, but I made friends with cat shifters wherever I went and so have always had a leg up on the human vets." He smiled at me, the light in his eyes soft and glowing.

"You really do love what you do, don't you?" I said.

He nodded. "Always have, and always will. Animals— the non-shifters—don't understand why they don't feel good, and this way, well, whether it's through a translator or through me, I can explain to some degree what's wrong, and I can convince them to let me treat them. I feel that this gives me the ability to help a lot more than a human vet can, just through the practical nature. You'd be surprised by how many shifters go into veterinary science."

I jumped up, walked around the table, and planted a soft kiss on his lips. "Thank you. Thank you for caring so much."

He pulled me onto his lap. "Thank you for acknowledging what I do as important."

We sat like that for a few moments until my stomach rumbled and I returned to my side of the table to finish my dinner. I told him about Ari and Peggin, and about the spirit shamans.

"I've heard of shifter Packs who are bound to the spirit shamans. They're legendary in our community, but there's little known about them and I've never met one." Killian finished off his sandwich and soup. "When are they due over?"

"At seven, which is why I fixed a dinner that was quick and easy." I sighed, leaning against the counter after I set the dishes in the sink. "Honestly, I have bigger concerns." I told him about the meeting with Tabitha. "I'm worried about the child. I do feel something's wrong there, but I'm afraid that if Tabitha gets too worried, she'll..."

"Hurt the baby because she thinks it isn't her Zoey?" Killian asked.

I nodded. "Yeah. She's panicking enough to where she talked to the doctor about it."

"I'm surprised they haven't sent a caseworker over there yet," Killian said. "They have to be so careful now."

"Maybe they have and she didn't tell us," I said. "I feel like she's leaving something out, but I can't just outright accuse her of lying."

"Can you just not take the case?"

I had thought about it, but then decided no, not when a child's life came into play. "I'll talk to Ari about it, and maybe I'll go talk to Millie. She understands the magical forces at work in this town. She won't outright dismiss Tabitha as a nutjob, but maybe making her aware of the potential problems would be a good idea." I let out a long sigh, wanting to change the subject. "So, when does Tally get into town?"

"Noon, I think. She'll come by the clinic and hang out with me there till after work. When will you get home?"

I shrugged. "I'll try to be home by six at the latest. We aren't on a huge case at work—mostly just tying up loose ends from the last one. Also, Hank's obsessed with sasquatch right now and has been exploring a few leads.

Tad wants to keep us clear on the chance that there's something for us to move on. Honestly, I don't look forward to meeting up with Mr. Congeniality."

"Bigfoot's dangerous and unpredictable, and the last thing in the world you need is to get into a confrontation with one of them."

I cocked my head. "Have you ever encountered one?"

"*Encountered* bigfoot? I was lucky to get out of the woods *alive* the one time I ran afoul one. I'm not joking—those creatures are fast, they're volatile, and they're clever. I accidentally hiked smack into one's territory a few years ago. I was alone—well, not exactly alone. A group of buddies and I went fishing for the weekend. We agreed to meet at Lake Wanetcha, a lake in northern California, and I was the first one there. I set up my tent and decided to gather some firewood."

"You had to watch out for mountain lions and rattlesnakes, didn't you?" While I couldn't pinpoint where Lake Wanetcha was, I had a pretty good idea of the rough geography.

"Oh, yes. Rattlers and scorpions and black widows, they all abound there. It was high summer, but the nights can get as cold as the days get hot. I wanted to make certain that we were prepared for the shift in temperature. If you forget to gather firewood until after dark, you're most likely going to get in trouble. So I left the campground and went into the surrounding forest to gather dry wood. I damned near got bit by a scorpion, too. I picked up a large piece of wood only to discover a nest of them beneath it."

"I'd have freaked," I said, grimacing. I liked the

outdoors and I enjoyed glamping—rather than camping—but scorpions and black widows were a solid *nope*.

He shuddered. "I love animals but I don't love beasties that are designed to kill me, and trust me, black widows and scorpions? They don't have much else on their minds. Anyway, so I was carrying the wood back to camp when I saw a scorpion crawl out from between two pieces of wood. I dropped the wood and shook the scorpion off my arm before it could bite me."

I nodded, not wanting to envision the encounter, but it was pretty easy to summon up a lot of images that I'd rather not imagine.

"Well, I was taking my time, picking the wood back up one piece at a time as I shook off any hitchhikers when I heard a noise nearby. I heard something rustling in the bushes. I thought maybe it was one of my buddies, so I called out, but no one answered."

"Why do I get the feeling this is one trip that didn't make your best-vacations list?"

Killian grinned. "Right. As I called out for my friends, the bushes parted and I thought I saw a very large bear. The next moment, I realized the bear was on its hind legs and it wasn't a bear, it was… It was shaped like a man but covered in fur. I guess if I had to describe him, I'd say he looked a lot like Chewbacca from *Star Wars*."

The thought of seeing a large, lovable Wookiee barging out of the forest both made me smile and chilled me to the bone, mostly because Wookiees weren't real, and sasquatch was.

"What happened?"

"He came after me," Killian said. "He came lurching out

and the moment he saw me, he started to run toward me. I took off. He was at least eight feet tall and naked, which is how I know he was a male. I didn't stick around to find out if he was friendly—when somebody is running full tilt your way, with bared, very sharp teeth, *you run*. He was tall enough that if he was any faster, he could have just tossed me over his shoulder. I've no doubt he would have carried me off to eat me. Or something equally as bad. But when he got close, he stopped, skidding to a halt. I turned around to see a mountain lion crouching behind me, growling."

My stomach lurched. "Talk about being caught between a rock and a hard place. What did you do?"

"Sasquatch turned tail and ran. The lion turned out to be another shifter who was hiking in the woods. He told me that sasquatches are terrified of the big cat shifter prides, and with good reason. They're like…mortal enemies or something. But he walked me back to the campsite and stayed with me until my buddies arrived. He warned us to stay in the campgrounds, not to go hiking around. And never go anywhere alone. We followed his advice and didn't see a single sign of bigfoot the rest of the weekend."

I sat back, thinking that if Tad suggested we go out camping in the woods looking for bigfoot, my first act would be to say no way, and then I'd tell him Killian's story, and if he still insisted, I'd drag Killian into work and tell him that Tad wanted me to go hunting for sasquatch.

"Well, that certainly helps me make up my mind about how involved I want to get in Hank's obsession. Why don't you tell him about your experience? He can use the input, and it might also forestall any unnecessary meetings in the wild."

"If you think it will help," Killian said.

"I do." The doorbell rang and I went to answer it while Killian finished rinsing the dishes and stacking them in the dishwasher. Ari and Peggin had arrived.

Peggin had changed into a pair of gauchos—straight out of the 1970s—and a V-neck sweater. She was also wearing a short rainproof jacket and a pair of very cute ankle boots that were meant for walking.

"You look ready to meet the woods," I said, suddenly thinking that maybe Killian's story was a good warning to us all. While I didn't think the Mystic Wood was home to sasquatch, the fact was, it *was* home to a number of unpredictable and erratic creatures and we were taking just as big of a chance heading into it at night as Killian had taken in the woods in northern California.

But I can't be afraid of everything, I thought. I wasn't even really *afraid* of the Mystic Wood, just wary. Rebecca was out there, for one thing, and while the little demon wouldn't come near a group of us, I had to bank on there being bigger, badder versions of her around.

Ari and Peggin came in, chattering away. For a moment, I felt a little excluded. Then I noticed that, while they seemed to be good friends, Ari held herself at a certain distance that she never did with me.

Calm down, I told myself. *She's still your best friend. Quit thinking she's going to dump you. She didn't when she got engaged, she's not going to now.*

Wondering where my sudden bout of insecurity came from, I forced a smile and led them into the kitchen, where I introduced Peggin to Killian. He was gracious to her, taking her hand when she offered it, and once again, something nibbled at the back of my mind as I scrutinized the look on his face.

What the hell?

"Ari, can I talk to you for a moment?" I asked, dragging her into the living room. When we were far enough from the kitchen that I knew neither Killian nor Peggin could hear us, I turned to her. "What's the deal with Peggin?"

"What do you mean—*oh*! I know what you're talking about," Ari said. "Don't worry about her. She's trustworthy. But she carries the energy of Aphrodite in all those bountiful curves. She's not exactly pledged to the goddess, but she seems to tap into the energy on a natural basis."

I stared at her, then shook my head. "I can't believe I didn't pick up on that before. The minute Killian said hello to her, I was immediately—"

"Worried he'd fall for her? Yeah, trust me, she's not bi, but when she met Meagan, I had that *same* insecurity. But you—you're a sex goddess now, remember?" She grinned.

I snorted. "Just because I misplaced a wish doesn't mean I'm a sex goddess. I just tapped into the energy a little more. And I seem to be getting a handle on it."

"Whatever the case, quit worrying. Besides, Peggin's taken and she's monogamous. She's involved with some inventor or artist, I guess you'd call him. His name is Dr. Divine. I met him once when I was over there and...let me just say, Peggin's far less vanilla than I am." Ari laughed and wrapped her arm through mine. "Come on, before they think we've skipped out for milkshakes or mocha."

We headed back into the kitchen, with me wondering why I was so touchy lately. I'd been insecure before in my life, mostly with Ellison, but here I was, acting like a teenager afraid she was going to lose her boyfriend and her best friend to the same person.

That's what happens when you love people, Esmara said. *You worry you'll lose them.*

Well, I know that, but… I paused.

Love people? Okay, I loved Ari. That I knew—she was my BFF and I wouldn't ever willingly give up that position in her life. But…Killian? He called me "love," but that was an endearment. And that was when I realized that, while we hadn't said the words yet, it felt like they were hanging there in the air.

I love you, I thought, looking at Killian. *I really do love you.*

And as soon as the realization came crashing in, I wanted to find a place to hide. I wasn't ready to face love again. I wasn't ready to face the heartaches and trials that went with it…was I? As my gaze settled on him as he stood there, talking to Peggin, I knew that I couldn't lie to myself. I *loved* Killian. And that shifted the game in so many ways.

Forcing a smile, I headed for the kitchen door, now eager to go hiking in the dark through a magical wood. It meant that I wouldn't have to sit with my thoughts, just yet. I wouldn't have to figure out whether I should say anything, to wonder what to do if he didn't return my feelings. And I wasn't ready to face the possibility that he might want to keep things casual.

As we headed across the yard, I heard myself talking, answering questions, but for the life of me, I couldn't tell you what the conversation was about.

CHAPTER FIVE

*T*he Mystic Wood had stood for hundreds, if not thousands of years. At one time, the glaciers rolled through the valleys, grumbled and groaned over the forests, bringing the long winter to the land. Seventeen thousand years ago, the Cordilleran Ice Sheet flowed through northwestern Washington, burying everything and everyone in a sheet of ice that was—in some places—estimated to be over three thousand feet deep.

The ice was so heavy that it weighed down the land, and that's how Puget Sound was formed. Eventually, as spring came to the earth again, the glaciers retreated, their fingers slowly withdrawing, leaving behind massive swaths of alluvial deposits—blankets of rocks covering hillsides—and channels where there had been no channels before.

During the rejuvenation of the world, the Mystic Wood had formed and the native peoples had returned to the area, and once again both the physical and the spiritual entities of the world walked the paths of the forests, dodging the quakes and volcanoes. The Cascades took over, the mountains of fire shifting the land as the tectonic plates twisted and fractured below the surface of the earth and water. As the bays formed and the ley lines harmonized, the Mystic Wood had gained its power, attracting beings of both shadow and light.

As we approached the tree line, the aura flared brighter. I wasn't sure if the others could see it, but I definitely could.

"Do you see it?" I asked.

"You mean the aura of the wood? I do," Ari said.

"I can't, but I can feel it," Peggin spoke up. "The woods out on the peninsula are deadly, filled with dangerous beings. This one feels different—crafty and cunning, potentially dangerous, but not in the same way. Our woods are older and darker than these, but these feel… more *magical* in a way."

"How so?" Killian asked.

"Whisper Hollow is a town of the dead, situated on the edge of the Veil. Moonshadow Bay's underlying energy feels magical, like it sits on the edge of a different realm. Do you have a lot of wood spirits here? Fae?"

I paused, cocking my head. "Fae? I know there are supposed to be Woodlings here, which I believe are part of the realm of Faerie."

"The Fae are glittering, clever creatures. But I think I'd rather have them than some of the creatures we have over there."

"January works for Conjure Ink," Ari said. "They investigate urban legends and other matters. You guys should go visit Whisper Hollow. Peggin's told me about some weird creepy critters over there that would be right up your alley." She flashed me a smile. "Why don't you talk to Tad about it?"

I wasn't sure how eager I was to spend time in a town that lived on the edge of the Veil. "I don't know...dealing with the dead isn't easy." I shook my head. "Although I *am* supposed to be learning how, according to Esmara—" I stopped as Peggin glanced at me, curiosity in her eyes.

"Who's Esmara?"

"She's my great-aunt. I'm from one of the witchblood families. In my family, we have the Ladies—the women of our bloodline come back and guide those of us still living. My great-aunt Esmara was assigned to me. I'm not sure *who* makes the assignments, but they figure it out together. My mother is with the Ladies now, so she'll eventually be someone's guide."

"Fascinating," Peggin said, and she sounded like she meant it.

We were at the tree line by then, and I paused. "All right, here we are. I don't recommend traveling off the path. Killian's a wolf shifter, so he can protect us against some of the creatures, but I haven't entered these woods in a long time and I'm not sure what we might find."

Ari turned to Peggin. "Not many people in town go into the woods here. Not without friends along with them. There are some beautiful campgrounds over east, near Mount Baker, and a campground down near the bay, but they aren't part of the Mystic Wood."

Peggin nodded. "The entire area—Western Washington in general—is steeped in magical energy. There are so many ley lines running through the area. Since both Whisper Hollow and Moonshadow Bay are built over the lines—over conjunctions of them, I believe—it's no wonder we have similar energies running through our homes."

She took a deep breath. "To be honest, I wanted to see your town after you told me about it, Ari. I have a friend back home who needs to move. Whisper Hollow is growing dangerous for her. But she's a shifter and she needs to find a place where she'll be comfortable. Her name is Mariana, and she's a bear shifter. I thought seeing that you're so close to the Mount Baker area, this might be a good home for her."

"Send her over," I said. "If she needs a welcoming place to live, then we're a good choice. Why is Whisper Hollow dangerous for her?"

"She's been marked by the Lady. Unlike *your* Ladies, ours is the Lady of the Lake. I was marked by her too, but my friends managed to remove the target from me. Don't ask how—it was a dangerous ritual. Unfortunately, I don't think Mariana would make it through the rites." Peggin took a deep breath, then nodded. "Yes, I think she'd fit in here."

I led the way into the Mystic Wood, armed with a flashlight. Daylight saving time had begun the night before—I hated it, but there was no getting around it—and so sunset was now at a little past seven instead of a little past six. But in the thick of the woods, it was dark and twilight cast its own glow across the wood.

The trees of the Mystic Wood were mixed—tall timber mixed with soft woods. Firs and cedar abounded, as they did everywhere on the coast of Western Washington, and interspersed among the conifers were maple and birch, alder and cottonwood. Huckleberry bushes were also beginning to leaf out, their leaves still tightly encased in

tiny buds, and the new growth on ferns was showing—
the coiled ends tightly wound. They would unfurl as
spring took hold, reaching out like lacey tentacles. The
skunk cabbage had bloomed early this year, the glossy
long leaves shimmering in the dim light. Their yellow
flowers hadn't fully opened, but when they did, they
would smell to high heaven—hence the name. But the
presence of skunk cabbage showed that our ecosystem
was still thriving, and it didn't smell quite as bad as it
sounded.

As we walked along the trail—which had been well
compacted over the years—to the sides I could hear whis-
pers and sense movement. I didn't say anything. It wasn't
wise to attract too much attention to oneself after dark.

I paused as we came to a fork in the trail. The side trail
—heading deeper within the wood—was narrow and
closed in. I shook my head and we continued along the
main route. To one side, I glimpsed a faerie ring—a circle
of *amanita muscaria*—the mushrooms known as fly agaric.
They were hallucinogenic, with their brilliant red tops
buttoned with white, but they were also considered toxic
when not prepared correctly. The Finns and Sami peoples
used them for vision quests. I left them alone because they
belonged to the Fae and I didn't relish stepping on toes by
disrupting a faerie ring.

As we drew deeper into the wood, the energy shifted
in a subtle but noticeable way. Every branch, bud, and
stone felt like it was crackling, and every tree seemed to
have eyes staring at us. The entire forest was alive, an
entity unto itself. I had read about massive fungi, whose
roots spread for miles belowground, the mushrooms and
toadstools popping up simply part of a much larger

organism. In fact, the biggest organism on the planet was one of the fungal colonies.

And that's what the Mystic Wood felt like—one massive entity that had thousands of avatars in the shapes of trees and bushes and stones.

"I've never felt anything quite like this," Peggin said in a hushed voice.

"There aren't many like it," I answered. "Oh, all forests have a sentience, a consciousness, but few are as aware and alert as the Mystic Wood. Be wary of anything you do in here—never start a fire where it could get out of control, and if you do start a fire, I recommend bringing your own wood. Take a piece from the forest and you risk enraging the tree spirits." I wasn't sure how I knew this, but the words sprang forth as if I had studied the woodland in depth.

Killian shivered. "There are all manners of creatures in here, but yes, I feel the nature spirits and the Fae are strong here. I've seldom had much to do with them—they are apart from even the Otherkin of this world—but I've encountered a few. In California, there are sacred spaces where they thrive, and they aren't very welcoming to humans or to most Otherkin."

Peggin nodded, pulling closer to me. I suppressed a smile. If she thought that I could protect her because I was taller, she was sadly mistaken. I did think it odd that she gravitated toward me instead of Killian, who was the obvious choice for someone to hide behind.

"What are you looking for?" I asked her. "Why did you want to come out here?"

She looked startled in the glow of the flashlight, but shrugged. "I don't know. It feels that if I find it, I'll know.

As I said, I came here to see Ari and check out the town for my friend. I think she'll do well here. But I feel like there's some sort of connection that I need to make. Maybe I've already made it," she said, pausing. With a glance at me, she added, "I want you to meet my BFF. I think you two would have a lot in common, even though you're vastly different in your abilities."

Be cautious. There's a point ahead on the path that you should not cross, Esmara said, interrupting my thoughts. *When you see the gold shimmer, turn around. Don't ignore my warning.*

"Hey, Esmara just warned me that we should turn around soon," I said. "When she's this adamant, it means trouble if I don't listen." It was right then that I saw what she had been talking about. A golden sheen flickered across the path like a beam of light. It shimmered, mesmerizing in its look, but the longer I stared at it, the more nervous it made me. "Let's go," I said, urging the others to turn around. "I'm not comfortable here."

"It's so pretty," Peggin said, moving forward.

I caught her by the arm as she neared the light. "No, don't cross it. I don't know what it is, but you need to stay away from it."

"Listen to January," Ari said. "There's something beyond the light that we don't want to waken."

As Peggin reluctantly turned away, I gave her a little shove and fell in behind her, Ari by my side. Killian brought up the rear. As we headed back the way we had come, I glanced over my shoulder. There, in the glow of the golden light, I caught sight of something watching us. It reminded me of a living statue created of twigs and branches. The eyes were glowing, and the creature had a small mouth, but when it smiled, I saw narrow, razor-sharp teeth. Whatever it was, I was grateful that it was on the other side of the light. It caught my gaze and gave me a bone-chilling smile.

I gasped and picked up the pace. "There's something behind the light. It feels like a curtain, so it's probably a vortex into a different realm, but I can guarantee that we do *not* want to meet whatever that thing is."

My voice must have contained the right amount of concern because Peggin and Ari picked up their pace as well, and we headed back along the path, which had suddenly taken on a darker tinge. Whatever that thing was, it made Rebecca the imp look like the Rebecca from Sunnybrook Farm. I said very little until we reached the edge of the woodland and once again, stepped into my yard.

Turning around, I scanned the tree line, looking for any sign that we had been followed. The entire forest was lit up now, and the energy that flared off of its aura reminded me of the aurora borealis.

Breathing deeply, I closed my eyes and felt for my wards. I had buried them deep, all along the boundaries of my property. Now, as I sought them out, the wall of protection shimmered up, standing strong at the borders of my land. The wards were throbbing, their energy gently pulsating through the night, and I let out a breath of relief.

"We're safe enough—as safe as we can be, in Moon-shadow Bay." I nodded toward the house. "Let's go inside."

After we shed our jackets and shoes, Ari helped me make raspberry mochas for everyone, and I found a box of doughnuts in the cupboard. We settled down around the kitchen table.

"So, did you find what you were looking for?" Ari asked.

Peggin shrugged. "I think I did…as I said, I wasn't even sure what I was searching for, but I'm good. I know what to tell my friend when I get home."

"What was that creature?" Killian asked.

I glanced over at him. "You saw it too?"

"The golden one? Yes. It was like nothing I've ever seen before. Was that the Rebecca spirit that you were telling me about?"

I shook my head. "Rebecca's an imp—a minor demon of sorts. Whatever this creature was, it wasn't anywhere near the same energy. I think it was Fae. I don't know what most of them look like, and I'm not sure I want to ever find out. But whatever it was, it was holding sway over that patch of land there, and the trail running through it."

"Do you mind if I give Kerris your phone number?" Peggin asked.

I shook my head. "No, I don't mind at all. I'd like to meet her. I'm intrigued now about spirit shamans and what they do. They aren't witchblood, are they?"

She shook her head. "No, they're not witchblood, not in the way you think of it. But they are born into a very few families. I'm surprised Moonshadow Bay doesn't have one. You must have a number of the dead returning here."

I shrugged. "Yeah, we do, but I guess we've never run into a problem before that required anything too drastic. I mean, I can exorcise some hauntings just fine. Others are more tricky. And spirit shamans can't do anything about the shadow people, can they? We have an overabundance of shadow people."

"Shadow people are frightening. We don't have as many." Peggin paused, then said, "So, if I tell my bear shifter friend to move here, will you show her around?"

I nodded. "Of course. Just tell Ari when she's coming and we'll help her get settled in."

The rest of the evening, we spent chatting about our respective towns, talking about spirits and denizens of the forests, and then Ari and Peggin left by ten.

Killian turned to me. "Peggin seems like a nice woman."

"Yeah, she does." I paused, then said, "I'm sorry, I feel like an idiot, but I have to tell you something. When I saw you talking to her—"

"You were jealous. You were afraid I'd make a play for her?" Killian said.

I nodded, blushing. "I don't usually act so insecure. I'm not sure why she affected me so much, except that Ari told me that Peggin embodies Aphrodite's energy."

"Well, rest your mind. She's pretty, yes, and I like my women with a little more meat on their bones, but she's not *you*, January. Not only that, but she's mated to someone else, and I don't make a play for women who are in a committed relationship. In my Pack, when you make a vow to someone, be it for the short term or long term, you keep it." He pulled me into his embrace, holding me closely.

"I promise you this, January Jaxson. So long as we're together, I will never cheat on you. I'm open-minded in terms of men and women being friends—some in my Pack are not—but I will never cross the line. If for some reason we don't work out, then I will end our alliance before I ever look at another woman. I give you my word of honor. Do you understand? You're my mate, and even though we don't know where this is going yet, I take that seriously."

I nodded. "I understand, and I promise you the same thing. After Ellison, it's hard to trust, but I know you enough to know that you take your honor seriously." And then I took a shaky breath and said the hardest words for me to say. "I believe you."

He kissed me then, low and deep, long and hard, and our bodies fit together snuggly, as though we were meant for one another.

"Do you want to stay the night?" I whispered, feeling him harden as he was pressed against me.

"I want to stay the night, yes, but I have to get up early for work tomorrow. I need a good night's sleep because I'm running a livestock clinic tomorrow, and that's hard physical labor, taking care of equines and bovines." He sighed, resting his forehead against mine. "But as soon as we have the chance, I will carry you off to bed and cover you with kisses."

Feeling absolutely cared for and adored, I nodded. I wanted to burst out with an "I love you," but this wasn't the time or place. It would keep, and hopefully I wouldn't just blurt it out without warning until we had more time to talk about it. I wanted to make certain I wasn't pushing things too fast, regardless of my feelings.

"All right then, Dr. O'Connell. Go home, and leave me alone in my bed," I murmured, teasing him.

"As long as nobody else but the cats shares it with you,"

he said. Giving me one more kiss, he gathered his coat and headed out the front door, over to his house.

As I locked up before going to bed, once again I stepped out onto the back porch. The Mystic Wood was lit up like a carnival, and as I watched the glowing aura of the trees, it occurred to me that I lived on the border to another world. And right now, it felt like something in that world was trying to creep out into mine.

CHAPTER SIX

I was running about fifteen minutes late by the time I got to work the next morning. First, my hair dryer had shorted out, then I had burned my breakfast—in the microwave, no less—and when I stopped for coffee and a replacement breakfast, I ended up behind a woman who couldn't make up her mind what she wanted. Her order seemed to take forever, and by the time I pulled through to pay for my sausage muffin sandwich and triple-shot mocha, I knew I'd never make it on time. So I parked in the coffee shop's parking lot and wolfed down my breakfast, licked my fingers before wiping them with a wet-wipe, and headed out at a sensible speed. Tad wouldn't care if I was a little late. He *would* mind if I got in an accident.

"Hey, sorry I'm late," I said. Everyone was gathered around the main table where we held our morning meetings.

"Sleep through the alarm?" Caitlin said.

I laughed, shaking my head. "No, hairdryer conked

out, I burned my breakfast in the microwave, and then got caught behind the slowest person in the world at the Java Junkie." I settled in at the table. "So, what's on the agenda today?"

In the few months since I had come to work for Conjure Ink, I'd become an integral part of the team, and I had found my niche. I got along with my coworkers *and* I enjoyed my job. That combination was rare in the work world.

"We're still on the hunt for sasquatch," Hank muttered, staring at a printout. "There have been new reports from up on Mount Baker. I'd like to schedule a trip up there so we can take a look around, but it's a little cold unless we take an RV."

Thinking back on my talk with Killian, I shifted uncomfortably. "Dude, I'm not thrilled about chasing the creature down, but Killian has quite a story, if you want to interview him. He got chased by one in the woods."

"Oh, sasquatch is volatile, for sure," Hank said, still staring at the photograph he had printed out. "But..." He shook his head. "Anyway, I'd like to schedule a trip up to Baker in May, when it's a little warmer."

"Go ahead and put it on the calendar. Three days, two nights. That's enough time to check out some of the reported areas." Tad glanced at me. "How's your spooky child case coming? Do you still need equipment?"

"To be honest," I admitted, "I've been thinking this may be more than Ari and I can handle."

"What's going on?" Wren asked.

I told them about Tabitha Sweet and her daughter. "There's definitely something odd going on, but whether it's caused by some kind of psychosis, or a possession, or...Tad suggested a changeling…I don't know. Ari and I wanted to go in there with a FLIR, an EMF, and a camera to see if we could catch anything on film." I paused. "I doubt if Tabitha can afford our fee, let alone Conjure Ink's fee, though."

"Why don't we do it as a pro bono case?" Tad said. "We're not doing anything else right now, except for the sasquatch hunt."

"You'd do that?" I asked.

Tad, who was the brains of Conjure Ink, had also built the company from scratch, funding it from the massive trust fund his parents had given him. When he came of age and in control of the funds, the first thing he did was to create the business and also started Urban Legends Inc., an umbrella group linking a number of paranormal investigations companies. All of the organizations worked together and shared information.

"Of course," he said, glancing at his calendar. "My family is noted for charity work, and I might as well continue on the tradition in the realm that I like to play in. Why don't you call her and ask if we can come out and check out the nursery."

I texted Ari, asking if she minded if Conjure Ink joined in the investigation, and she texted back that she was fine with that—she was feeling trepidatious about the case anyway, given how wary Tabitha was of the child.

"Ari is good with CI coming in, so let me give Tabitha a call," I said, moving away from the table where we were all gathered.

"Hello? January?" She sounded relieved. "I wasn't sure if you'd call me back."

"Hey, my company that I work for—Conjure Ink—

would like to come investigate what's going on in your house. We have the equipment to do so, and Ari and I feel you'd benefit from a bigger crew coming in. We'll do it pro bono, no worry about a fee."

She hesitated, then in a burst of relief that was tangible in her voice, said, "Yes, thank you. Can you come over today? I'm getting more and more creeped out by that...*thing*. It's becoming harder to force myself to feed her when I know in my heart she's not Zoey. I just... It's hard for me to touch her."

"We'll be out today," I said. "I'll text you when I know what time." I hung up, shuddering. If she stopped feeding the baby, she was on slippery ground. We'd have to keep a close eye on the case and bring in Millie at the first sign of neglect.

I turned to the others. "Tabitha is grateful for our help. But I can't emphasize enough that we're on dangerous ground. She's convinced that the baby isn't her child— that Zoey is...some sort of replacement. I'm worried that she'll neglect the baby if this goes on much longer. She just told me she's finding it difficult to even feed the child, so we're near the edge of neglect and endangerment already."

"Do you feel she's mentally unstable?" Tad asked.

I thought for a moment, wanting to make sure that I had a handle on my instincts. "As crazy as she sounds, I think there *is* something going on with the child. There *is* something creepy about Zoey, but I'm not sure why or what."

"Hank, what should we take with us?" Tad asked.

Hank frowned, tapping his fingers on the table. "Well,

a FLIR, EMF, security cameras just like January was going to. So, did the child test out as human?"

"As far as the doctor could see, but maybe we should bring in Dr. Fairsight," I said. Dr. Fairsight specialized in treating Otherkin, so there was the chance she might find something a human doctor couldn't.

"Good idea." Tad glanced at the clock. "Wren, call her and ask her if she can meet us today over at Tabitha's house. Do that now while we wait."

I felt a little odd, handing one of my first cases that Ari and I had taken on over to Conjure Ink, but it wasn't a simple haunting and it just felt wiser to bring in a team when the problem was bigger than expected.

Wren put in a call to the doctor and within ten minutes, she agreed to meet us at one P.M. over at Tabitha's. I called Tabitha back and told her we'd be there a little after noon. That would give us some time to set up before Dr. Fairsight arrived.

The rest of the morning we returned to cataloguing bigfoot reports, though Tad asked me to check out the equipment to make certain it was charged and ready. I actually didn't mind. It meant they trusted me, and that I was actually part of the team instead of just the "new employee." I went through the store room, wiping dust off cameras and testing the batteries to see if anything needed to be charged.

Twenty minutes later, I had gathered what we needed, made sure it was all in working order, and packed it up in the equipment bag. I returned to the main office. "We're set to go. I had to put three of the cameras to charge, but everything else was full of juice."

Tad glanced at the clock. "We'll leave in an hour. We'll

probably miss lunch, so why don't you run over to Jacko-Burger. Everybody, what do you want?"

I pulled up the Jacko-Burger app and began entering orders for pickup. When everybody had finished placing their orders—except for Wren, who unfailingly brought her lunch—I grabbed the company credit card and headed across the parking lot to the fast food joint.

Our orders were waiting. I paid for the food and then, stuffing the bags in two large canvas food totes, I returned to the office. As I handed out the food, we settled around the main table. Wren put up the "Ring the bell" sign at the reception desk and joined us.

"Say, have any of you ever heard of Whisper Hollow?" I unfolded the foil on my double cheeseburger. I had a strawberry shake to go with that, and a small side of fries.

Tad swiveled to stare at me. "Whisper Hollow? Why?"

"Because I met someone from there this weekend. She's apparently the best friend of the local spirit shaman. She told me a little about Whisper Hollow and it seems like it would be just the place for us to explore—"

"Before you go further," Tad said, "My parents were *born* in Whisper Hollow. They left shortly after they got married. My father had several run-ins with the Lady and she marked him. He doesn't dare go back."

I stared at him. "No wonder you grew up so fascinated by things like urban legends. So, have *you* ever been over there?"

He shook his head. "I want to, but my father's afraid that I inherited his mark. Until I know for sure, they asked me to stay away." He paused, then met my gaze and I could see the warring emotions there. "I want to go. I feel sometimes like the town is calling to me, but there's part of me that's worried that I'd be walking into my own death."

"Does the Lady really kill?" I hadn't had time to do any research on everything that Peggin had told me about.

"Oh, she claims whoever she wants. Most often, she doesn't give them back. But now that you mention it, it would be helpful to have a contact over there, in case we ever get called in on a case." Tad went back to his burger.

Hank glanced at Tad, then back at me. "It's better we stay in Moonshadow Bay. While the Mystic Wood can be dangerous, it's a different kind of danger than Whisper Hollow, and Moonshadow Bay is an easier place to stay alive." He gave me a slight shake of the head that warned me to change the subject.

With one last glance at Tad, I shifted gears, telling them everything I could remember about what Tabitha had told me.

"Tad, you mentioned a changeling. How does that happen?" I asked.

He cleared his throat. "Well, first, it means that the Fae exchanges one of their own children for a human child. Their baby is given a glamour to where they are essentially a replicant of a human child down to the very DNA. They swap the children, and steal the human child away to their realm."

"Why do they do this?" I asked.

"I don't think anybody really knows," he said. "Usually the duplicates are really identical. I don't know how they do it other than glamour, but..."

"Possession?" Caitlin asked.

Hank shook his head. "No, possession is usually limited to spirits. Changelings are *physically* swapped out.

The replica is unidentifiable from the original except for the hatred of iron. Touch iron to the child's skin. If it's Fae, if it's from their world, it should scream."

I frowned. That sounded cruel. "Do you have to touch them with it, or can you just bring it near them?"

"That I don't know. I have an iron chain in my truck I can bring," Hank said.

"You're *not* hitting the child, and with a chain no less!" Caitlin jumped up, staring at Hank with a look of horror on her face.

"Of course not," he said, snorting. "You just lightly touch the iron against their skin. In fact, if they're extremely sensitive, just bringing the chain inches away might produce a reaction. And with the Fae, there's no way to describe their revulsion to the metal."

We finished up lunch and Hank glanced over the equipment. He gave me a thumbs-up and we stopped at his truck to gather the chain, then everybody piled in the van to head over to Tabitha's.

As we approached the small bungalow, my mood began to sink. I still had the premonition that somehow, this was going to end up badly, and I didn't want to be witness to the fallout I could foresee happening.

"What's wrong?" Caitlin asked. We were sitting together in the back of the van, near the surveillance equipment. Hank rode shotgun with Tad. Wren, of course, stayed at the office. Given she was the reception-ist, she seldom went out on investigations.

"I don't know. Since Ari and I went there yesterday, I've felt gloomy and moody." I glanced back at the men, then lowered my voice. "I think that I'm afraid Tabitha is just mentally disturbed and that she's going to hurt the baby. I *know* there's something odd there—and Zoey *did* make me uneasy, but sometimes people just do that. And suggestibility can go a long way."

Caitlin sighed. "I know what you mean. Sometimes people think they're being psychically attacked, but they're just having a run of bad luck. It's easier to have someone to blame than face the fact that you might be causing the problems yourself. Or that...well...shit just happens sometimes."

"Tabitha's pediatrician told her that Zoey's fine. The child looks like she's in the picture of health. I mean, if the baby was ailing, maybe Tabitha would be looking for something to blame. But Zoey's strong and healthy." I shrugged. "I don't know. Something about this case just doesn't sit well with me." I shrugged, leaning back in my seat. Caitlin had a moody look of her own. "Are you okay?"

"Well, I can tell you, this weekend didn't sit well with me, either." Caitlin stared down at her hands. "Arlo came out point-blank and demanded we set a date for the wedding." She pressed her lips together, shaking her head.

Arlo was Caitlin's fiancé. When she was young, her parents had arranged a marriage to Arlo Wondersong, another bobcat shifter who was near Caitlin's age. She liked the guy, but she wasn't *in* love with him. If she broke the engagement, her family would be dishonored among their Pride, and she would be the reason. So Caitlin had kept the engagement going as long as she could in hopes that something would intervene, but there was no deus ex machina reaching its hand down from the heavens. If she didn't do something soon, she'd either have to marry him or run away at the altar. Neither option seemed preferable to defying her family while she had the chance to get out.

"You *have* to do something, Caitlin." I knew that Caitlin had fallen hard for Tad, and I suspected he felt something for her too, but he was a standup guy and he wouldn't go after her while she was engaged.

"Seriously, you're telling me? I *know* I have to do something. When he told me last night that we had to set the date and that his mother was getting concerned, all I could see was a string of years and kids stretching out in front of me. Arlo's nice, but the thought of…" She blushed, then lowered her voice even more. "The thought of letting him touch me makes me queasy. I want my first time to be with someone I'm attracted to."

I stared at her, not quite grasping what she was saying, but then it hit home. "You're…a *virgin*? You and Arlo haven't…"

"No, we haven't. Thank gods my shifter Pride is old-fashioned, so I could get away with telling him I wanted to wait until marriage. But now he's getting impatient and his mother's getting pushy and his family is getting together with my family to discuss the wedding this week. I can't, January." She glanced furtively toward Tad, who was oblivious to our conversation as he drove the van toward Tabitha's. "I just… I can't."

"Then you have no choice. You have to tell him that you're not in love with him. You owe it to him to be honest and let him move on with his life. But to do that, you're going to have to face disappointing your family." I wanted her to be sure when she made her choice. "Can you face telling them you don't want to marry him, more than can you face living with Arlo as a husband?"

She gave me a forlorn look. "I guess I have no choice. I don't love Arlo and I can't imagine letting him touch me. I tried, I really did. I tried to get on board with the whole thing, but…"

"But…your heart isn't there."

"No," she said, a bitter note in her voice. "And I resent being put in this position. If I follow my truth, I'll dishonor my family and probably be kicked out of the Pride. If I go along with what they want, I'll be miserable for the rest of my life. And I *know* myself. I'm not going to magically fall in love with someone just because he puts a ring on my finger. It's looking a lot like a lifelong prison sentence."

I tried to think of a way to make things easier. "Would you like me there for moral support?"

She laughed, a sour tinge to her voice. "Oh, January, you're a good friend, but you have no clue what you're volunteering for. No, it's better if you don't get involved. My mother would blame you for me changing my mind. She just can't fathom someone not doing their duty by the Pride. I guess I should rent a place in town because the moment I tell my parents, I'll be out on my ass. I live in one of the dormitories on Pride land—they're kept for those who are arranged to marry, or for those who are making the transition to living on their own."

I took her hand and gave it a squeeze. "If you need someplace to stay, you can always crash at my place. I have a guest room, you know. So don't let that stop you."

"Oh, it's time I found a place of my own. I have enough money. If I hadn't been supposed to marry Arlo, I would have moved away already. Thing is, this is going to drive my sisters crazy—I have two and I'm the eldest. This will upset their lives too. Neither of them can marry until I do. It's different for boys, but for girls—if I walk away, one of two things will happen. One, my sisters will be prevented from marrying until the Alpha proclaims them free from the restriction. Or two, my parents will immediately disown me, which will mean that I don't exist in the Pride's eyes and therefore, the next-eldest sister will move into the eldest position."

Caitlin's bobcat shifter pride seemed very restrictive to me.

"How does that make you feel?" I asked.

"Sad. But it's the most likely scenario." She leaned back in her seat. "Well, I'd better get used to being alone, because I certainly won't have a family after this. Not unless I marry outside of the Pride."

"You'll have us," I said. "You'll have Tad and Hank, Wren and me. We'll be there for you."

Caitlin caught my gaze and gave me a sad little smile. "Thank you," she said. "I appreciate that." As she glanced again toward Tad, I thought that this was the best thing that could happen, given the circumstances. After she told her parents, she would be free to pursue a relationship with a man who was hungry for love, whom she was already interested in. I had a feeling she and Tad would do well together.

"We're here," Tad called back. "I'll park and then, January, why don't you lead us in since you already know her."

Hank glanced back at us. "Whoa, you two look serious. Who died?"

I glanced at Caitlin, then shook my head. "Girl talk. Just girl talk."

Tad eased into a parking spot. As we headed out of the van, I glanced over at Tabitha's bungalow. It still looked neat and tidy outside, but the cloud was back, and I dreaded going inside. Resigned to a gloomy afternoon, I led them up the walk, to the door.

CHAPTER SEVEN

Tabitha looked even more frazzled than she had the day before. She let us in.

"All right, do you mind if we set up some equipment?" I asked her. "We also have another specialist coming in about an hour. She's a doctor and she'll examine Zoey, looking for...well...things other than what a normal doctor looks for. She specializes in Otherkin." I sat down with Tabitha while the others unpacked our gear.

She gave me a long look that told me she didn't fully understand, but she nodded anyway. "Where's your friend?"

"Ari? She had to work today. These are my coworkers at Conjure Ink." I introduced everyone. "You're in good hands. We do this for a living—investigate things like this." I paused, and she slowly relaxed. "You have to tell us the truth, though. Have you been feeding Zoey and changing her? Have you been hugging her?"

Tabitha bit her lip. "I've fed her and she's clean...but spending time with her is starting to be difficult. She's..."

"Not your baby, I know. But you have to take care of her, regardless. The police could take her away for good—and if she really *is* Zoey and something's just preventing you from seeing that, you could lose your daughter permanently." Sometimes, it was just better to be blunt.

Tabitha let out a long breath. "All right. I understand what you're saying."

"Good. Now I'm going to go help them examine the nursery and surrounding area. Why don't you go in your kitchen and have a cup of tea?"

As I gave her a little push toward the kitchen, Caitlin said something behind me. I waited until Tabitha was out of sight to turn around.

"That was difficult," I said, lowering my voice. "We'd better find something soon, or she's going to lose that baby and eventually, she'll regret it." I made my way over to Caitlin's side. She was standing in the hall. "What did you find?"

"Look at this," she said, holding out the EMF. The needle was off the charts. "There's so much electromagnetic energy here, it's crazy. This alone could be driving her to think Zoey's not hers."

"But where's it coming from? Something has to be causing it. Maybe the microwave or her computer are producing too many electromagnetic waves somehow?"

"I thought that at first, but look. Follow me." She walked into the kitchen toward the microwave and the levels began to fall to normal range. Caitlin led me back to the living room and over to the computer. The computer also showed a moderate level, but it wasn't spiking up either. So the high readings weren't due to either appliance, but something else.

"Which way is the kid's room?" she asked.

"Near where you were standing in the first place." I pointed to the hall. "The nursery is the first room there, on the right." As I led her over toward Zoey's room, I watched the PK reader, and as we approached Zoey's room, the spikes returned, higher than before.

"Cripes," I whispered, staring at the meter. "This is…"

"Off the charts. Hank, come over here, please." Caitlin held out the reader and he scrutinized it.

"Shit, that's…"

"I know," Caitlin said. "All right, what should we do first?"

"Try the iron trick," I said. "Though we're going to want to hook up the camera in the nursery so we can see if it will catch anything. What about the FLIR?"

"We can't use it until it's dark," Hank said. "Can Zoey get out of her crib and potentially hurt herself by knocking over any of the equipment?"

I shook my head. "I don't think so. She didn't look capable of it yesterday."

"I'll go ask," Caitlin said, heading for the kitchen.

I watched her go, then turned back to Hank. "Shall we go ahead and set everything up?" I didn't want to go back in the baby's room. I didn't want to see Zoey again, but this was my job and sometimes you had to do things you didn't want to. Hank gathered up the bags of equipment and I followed him into the nursery.

Immediately, I felt like I was being watched as I stood in the door, staring at the baby. Zoey was asleep, and in her slumber she looked angelic, but there was still something behind the surface, something that felt wary and shrewd. I tried to harness my fear and slowly stepped into the room, approaching the crib.

Hank started to set up a security camera where she couldn't reach it, even if she somehow managed to get out of the crib. When he finished, I leaned over the railings. Zoey shifted in her sleep and then, very slowly and deliberately, she opened her eyes and fastened her gaze on me. Without a word, she smiled—and not in that goofy baby smile way, but a crafty, sly smile.

"Crap, did you see that?" I asked.

"I got it on tape, yes. Here, let's try the chain."

I walked over to him and he handed me a small iron chain. I turned back, steeling myself. As I neared the crib, Zoey pulled herself into a sitting position and stared at me, her eyes wary now rather than sneaky. I reached down into the crib, not touching her, but with the chain in hand, and as I came within a few inches of her, she suddenly let out a long hiss and screamed at the top of her lungs. Her eyes flashed, turning a brilliant green before settling back down to baby blue.

I quickly pulled the chain away from her. "Well…"

"That went better than I expected," Hank said.

Zoey began to cry, tears running down her cheeks. I bit my lip, feeling horrible. Tossing the chain to Hank, I leaned in and lifted her out of the crib, cuddling her close.

"I'm sorry, I didn't mean to scare you. I'm sorry—" I paused as she quieted down, sniffling. There was an odd smell to her—it wasn't bad, but it reminded me of green apples and moss. "Who are you?" I asked, holding her out to get a good look at her. "Whose child are you?"

Hank was standing beside me. "We'd better put her

down again. But at least we know she can't stand the presence of iron."

"Yeah," I murmured. "I wish we hadn't needed to do that." Pausing, I thought it better to discuss the matter out of her earshot. "I'll meet you in the living room."

As we exited the bedroom, I glanced over to find Tad staring at me. I crossed over to him. "Dude, that kid's freakshow scary. I'm talking *Children of the Corn* scary. She reacted to the iron. I didn't even touch her with it, but she screamed bloody murder."

"Then she could easily be Fae. And they can take on an almost fool-proof glamour." He motioned for me to sit on the sofa. "Why don't you start monitoring the security camera."

Caitlin, who was already watching, glanced up as Tabitha entered the room, mug of tea in hand.

"Did I hear…her…scream?" Tabitha asked.

"Yes, but she's fine. She's not hurt."

"All right…" Tabitha looked harried and tired and confused. "Oh, I forgot to ask, do you want anything to drink or eat?"

"That's fine, Tabitha. Sit down and relax while we do the work." As I sat on the sofa, I slid off my boots. "Do you mind if I sit cross-legged?" I asked.

Tabitha shook her head. "I do it all the time."

I crossed my legs and moved the cart with the monitors on it to where it was directly in front of me. Hank would set up other surveillance cameras around the house and outside, and we'd stay for at least four or five hours. I must have looked tense, because Tad rested his hand on my shoulder.

"Take it easy. We can only go so fast. There's no way to rush this."

I glanced up at him. "You really are a good boss. I'm just nervous. When the baby screamed—and I just held the chain near her—it startled the hell out of me." I forced myself to take a deep breath and let it out slowly, then sat back, watching the monitor.

Zoey was asleep, looking cherubic, but then, within a few minutes, her eyes opened. She pulled herself to a standing position, holding on to the side of the railings, as she looked around the room, and then let out a laugh that chilled me to the core, a full-fledged *I'm going to get you* laugh. It rebounded through the room, far too deep for a child's lungs.

"That's no baby," I said, pointing to the camera. There was a shadow on the wall, thrown by the baby, and it wasn't at all the same shape. It seemed bipedal, but the shape was odd, though I couldn't quite point out why.

"You're right." Tad leaned forward. "What is that?"

"She can't be a shifter—even shifters throw the shadow of whatever alt-form they're currently in. Tell me more about changelings. How does it work?"

"From what I know, the Fae take human children and leave duplicates in their place. That's one of the reasons I asked about the possibility—the duplicate will resemble the missing child in every way, down to their DNA. It's as though the Fae are able to clone the child through their glamour magic. But the soul, the spirit, is the Fae child."

"Why do they do this, and how does the glamour break? Do you know? Is there any time when you can see through it?" I had very little to do with the Fae, but it seemed as though Tad had far more knowledge than I did.

"Yeah, there is. I remember reading stories about cases where changelings were involved. I'll have to look them up again, but I seem to remember hearing that the shadow can't lie and will give away the creature. Let me look it up again."

As he tapped away on his laptop, I gestured for Caitlin to take over watching while I crossed the room to sit by Tabitha. "I'm sorry we don't have a simple answer."

She gazed into my eyes, looking worn and weary. "Thank you. You're the first ones to take my concerns seriously. The doctor thinks I'm nuts, I know that. And so did everybody else I talked to. To be honest, I don't feel safe with...whatever it is in my house."

"When did you notice a difference?"

"About two weeks ago. It was the nanny's day off, so I took her on a walk to the park. She was in her stroller."

I perked up. So there *was* a defining moment. That could shed light on the issue. "Tell me everything you remember about that outing."

"We went to Thimbleberry Park—it's right next to the Mystic Wood. It was chilly but the sun was shining, and it was such a beautiful day that I wanted to get out. I was sitting on a bench and Zoey was in her stroller. Then..." She paused. "You know, I had forgotten all about this. I don't know how, but it just slipped my mind. I heard a child crying. It sounded like she had been hurt. I mean, really crying—you know, the 'Oh shit, did they break their arm?' kind of cry. I looked around and saw what I thought was a child sitting just inside the tree line. No other adult was around. It was only a few yards away, and I didn't want to leave her there if she had truly broken her arm or something like that. So I ran over there to check on her."

"And what happened then? Was she hurt?"

"She...wasn't even there. I got there, and there was no child in sight. I looked around, but she had vanished. It confused the hell out of me, but there was absolutely no one there. So I went back to Zoey, who was still in the stroller. The park suddenly felt darker... It made me nervous, so I left. When we got home, I thought I noticed something about Zoey. She seemed different. But I blew it off as a result of the odd encounter in the park. After that, though, Zoey didn't seem like herself. The nanny got spooked because of her—even though she gave me a different reason for leaving, I know it was because of Zoey. I took her to the doctor, but he said she was fine. I called the police, but they just acted like I was hysterical. So I tried to ignore it, but then I saw your card and thought I'd call you."

Crap. The Mystic Wood—anytime that copse was involved, something odd was sure to follow. I turned back to Tad, who had been listening even while he was searching on his phone.

He paused, then looked up at Tabitha. "Tell me something. How long were you there? How much time passed between when you went over to check out the little girl, and when you arrived back at the stroller?"

Tabitha frowned. "That's the odd thing. I went to the park during the early afternoon. I swear we can't have been there more than half an hour before that incident occurred. I arrived at the park at two o'clock. When I got home, it was nearly five. It takes me ten minutes to drive to Thimbleberry Park. So where did most of those three hours go?"

So we had missing time along with the event. "And

you didn't make any other stops on the way there or home?"

Tabitha shook her head. "No, I didn't."

Tad motioned to me. "I'm sending you some information via text. Take a look at the links."

I pulled out my phone and waited for his texts to come through. The links led me to stories about changelings—and almost all of the documented cases involved time loss and memory loss components. Each one seemed to mirror Tabitha's experience in terms of everything being fine, then some event where they had been separated from their baby for a time, and boom, the baby didn't seem the same afterward. I wanted to ask Tad what the end result was, but I worried that if it were bad, Tabitha would overhear and fret.

"Tad, can we chat in the kitchen?" We entered the kitchen and moved away toward the outer wall so that we were out of Tabitha's sightline and earshot. I sat down at the kitchenette table.

"What happened in those cases? What was the end result?"

"In two of the cases, the changelings just up and died on the couple. When they died, they turned back into their Woodling forms. There was one case where the mother went nuts and beat the child to death—again, it changed back into its natural form and she was acquitted when the court wasn't able to produce a corpse of the actual child."

"How long before it reverted to its natural shape?"

"It was on the morgue table, and the coroner was about to autopsy the child. The judge gave her a stern warning, but there was nothing else he could do. Without

a body, they had no case. They searched for her child—
she had been begging them to do something because she
was convinced her child was missing—but they never
found anything. In other cases, the changelings grew up
and then vanished. A couple went missing as teens, while
others managed to stick around till their early twenties
and then vanished."

"What do the Fae want with the human children?"

"I don't know. Nobody seems to know, though there
are theories on the subject. You might ask Rowan—she
probably knows more than me." Tad paused, then said,
"You do realize this case is likely to end in a bad way?
Either Tabitha will emotionally distance herself from the
child because she doesn't believe it's her daughter, or
she'll hurt the girl. Or abandon her."

I jerked my head up. "Why do you say that?"

"Because, in almost 80 percent of the cases involving
suspected changelings, the end result involves some sort
of heartbreak. The original children are never seen again.
The parents either go crazy because they are convinced
the child isn't theirs—and rightly so—so they hurt the
changeling, or they abandon it. Even if we prove that little
girl is a changeling, which is hard to do, then what next?
The DNA will still say it's Zoey."

"Way to make a bad situation darker, dude," I said, but
gave him a soft smile. "I'm already frustrated. I can't
imagine how Tabitha feels. And yet…"

"Yet, there's a part of you that believes that it's actually
Zoey and that Tabitha is overreacting?"

I nodded. "I hate that I feel that way, but even with
everything I've seen, there are so many other possible

explanations. So, what do we do? What good is it if we prove this isn't Zoey?"

"It's not going to help anyone, really. But we can't let that stop us." Tad slid up on the table next to my chair, swinging his legs as he stared toward the living room. "January, do you know what my first experience with the paranormal was?"

I shook my head. "I don't think you told me."

"My grandmother died. I loved her so much—she was the world to me. My parents were loving, but distant. But Nannie? She was always there. Until she wasn't. I was eleven, and she died, and I felt abandoned. So, one night, I was really missing her and I sat on my bed and begged her to come back. And she did."

"Oh hell, that must have been a shock."

"It was. She was standing there, looking a lot like she had when I last saw her, but she was mad as hell at me. She gave me a scolding I never forgot. She warned me never to call back the dead, not unless I knew exactly what I was doing. She said there were a lot of dangerous spirits out there, which scared me even more because I was worried about her. Then she told me, *Tad, there are some situations you just can't win. There are some circumstances where you'll have to just suck it up and move on.* And then she vanished for good."

I tried not to laugh, but the image of Tad's grandmother's ghost scolding him was too much. "It sounds to me like she didn't stop being your grandmother when she died."

"True, and I took what she said to heart. I felt better, seeing she was still...I'd use the word *alive*, but that's not correct. That she still existed, I suppose. And I suppose that's the day I became a realist rather than an optimist."

"What do you mean?"

"I leaned on her advice when the bullies in high school picked on me. There was no way to win. If I tried to outwit them, it just made them angrier. If I brought in help, they'd just wait until they caught me alone. I did my best to dodge them, and when they did catch me, I practiced non-resistance as best as I could. I think that was actually a deciding factor in them finally leaving me alone."

"Oh?" I could easily imagine Tad being picked on in high school. He was lean, short, and a brilliant geek. The perfect bully magnet.

"Yeah, it's like…when I stopped resisting, they got bored and left me alone. I found my salvation in choosing inaction."

"Isn't that a form of Buddhism?"

"You're thinking about non-resistance, and yes, that's a tenet of some forms of Buddhism. Anyway, I've discovered that when you don't set yourself up for disappointment, it's easier to deal with when it comes." He added, "I don't think Tabitha wants to hear my story or would understand how it applies to her, but in this case, her best bet is to accept the situation and find a way to make it work for her, or to give the child up. Because chances are good the real Zoey will never appear again."

I didn't like fatalism, but I also saw Tad's point. Beating your head against a brick wall didn't work very well, and while I was a stubborn woman, even I knew when it was time to throw in the towel and give up. But I didn't feel it was that time for Tabitha, not yet.

"Has anybody ever contacted the Fae in the Mystic Wood? The Woodlings?"

Tad gave me a sharp look. "Not the best idea, January."

"Maybe not, but if there's a reason they're swapping children, we should at least know why." I paused, thinking of my trip into the wood the night before. "I think I actually saw a Woodling last night."

"What?" Tad glanced at me. "They're so rare that almost nobody ever sees them."

I told him about our sojourn into the wood, and the creature I had seen in the glowing light. "It was odd, humanoid but definitely in no way human. It reminded me…I don't know, of a person made of branches, or like… oh, you know, something made of Popsicle sticks that have been glued together."

"You need to be cautious. If they know you saw one of them, there's a chance that they'll come after you to make certain you don't talk about it." As Tad slid off the table, Caitlin shouted for us. Our conversation finished, Tad and I hurried in to see what was going on.

CHAPTER EIGHT

*T*abitha was on her feet, looking concerned. She watched as we ran over to Caitlin's side.

Caitlin was pointing to the screen. "Look at this!"

Tad and I crowded behind her, and Hank came running from down the hall where he had been staked out, outside the nursery door. We jockeyed for position to see the screen and then, as we watched, I felt something lurch in the pit of my stomach.

There, on the screen, Zoey was shifting form. She seemed to be having some difficulty doing so—her face was scrunched up like she was trying to go to the bathroom—and she was holding herself up by the railing on the crib. But then, as we watched, the air around her sparkled and she morphed into a different shape, very similar to the one I had seen in the Mystic Wood.

"Damn, that's one of them. I think that's a Woodling," I said, trying to keep my voice low.

But Tabitha pushed her way through to where she could see the monitor. She took one look at the Zoey-substitute and let out a cry, her hand flying to her mouth in shock. "Where's…that's not Zoey! I told you that…*thing*…isn't my daughter."

"I know, and now we have proof. I think. Did we manage to catch the transformation?" I asked, looking at Caitlin.

She nodded. "Yeah, I did record it. Whatever that creature is—"

At that moment, the doorbell rang, startling us all.

"Oh, that's probably Dr. Fairsight," I said, running to answer the door. Sure enough, it was. "Come with me," I said, skipping the small talk.

Dr. Fairsight was a moderately tall woman, whose golden blond hair was cut in a short layered style. It looked natural rather than out of a bottle, and her eyes were a deep chocolate brown. She was sturdy but proportioned, and wore narrow black rectangle-framed glasses. She was dressed in a pair of linen trousers, and was wearing a pale blue blouse beneath her white lab coat. She followed me back to the setup where we were all watching the monitor. "What am I looking at—oh my," she said. "I haven't seen one of *them* in a long time."

"That was Tabitha's little girl until a few minutes ago. We weren't sure if the baby was possessed or what, but now we're thinking changeling."

"How can we keep the creature from changing back—" I paused again as the window in Zoey's room began to open.

What the hell? A larger figure who looked similar to the young Woodling crept in and swept up the baby. She reminded me of some woodland sculpture in motion as she held the baby to her breast. She held it tenderly, glowing eyes soulful and sad as she rocked the child in her arms. Then, she happened to look over toward the camera. The next moment, she hissed, placing the child back in the crib. As she backed away toward the window, the young Woodling began to scream, holding out her arms. The mother gave one last frantic look at the camera, then toward her baby, and darted out the window, leaving the child behind.

Hank raced down the hall. I followed along with Tabitha and the doctor as Tad and Caitlin headed out the door to see if they could head the Woodling off at the pass.

As we entered the nursery, the child looked at us, holding out her arms, crying. She began to shimmer, transforming back into Zoey as we surrounded the crib and turned on the light.

"Well, *that* was unexpected," I said.

Tabitha, however, surprised me. She bit her lip, staring at the child, then walked over to the crib and picked up the baby. "Did your mother leave you? You miss her, don't you? I'm sorry. It's okay…it's all right."

As she began to soothe the child, I glanced over at Tad, bewildered. The doctor shook her head as I opened my mouth to ask Tabitha what she was doing. A few moments later, the child had calmed down and Tabitha reluctantly gave her over to the doctor to examine.

We moved back into the living room, where I turned to Tabitha. "I thought…"

"I know, but when I saw that…I guess it was the mother…looking so forlorn when she had to leave her child… No mother should have to leave her child behind. Something must have forced her hand. I know that I'll do anything I can to get my Zoey back," she said, tearing up. "But now that I've seen what's going on, I can't just ignore the baby. She needs a mother."

Ah, the hormones had kicked in and the mothering gene had come out full force. Which was probably the best thing that could happen for the Woodling child.

"Sit down, it's been an eventful afternoon." I guided her to a chair. "First, do you understand what's happened?"

She shook her head. "Zoey's missing. That child… creature…in there isn't my baby. I'm not crazy!"

"They're called Woodlings. They're members of the Fae race. There's a wide diversity among the Fae, but the Woodlings seem to live here in Mystic Wood. I don't know if they exist elsewhere," I said.

Tabitha frowned. "I thought Faeries were…like the children of gods. You know, the Tootha…"

"Tuatha de Dannan? Yes, some of them are, but there are as many variants in the Fae race as there are in… well…cat breeds, or dog breeds. They're more diverse than human ethnicities." I was doing my best to recall what I had learned about cryptobiology in high school.

"I see," she said. A moment later she asked, "So they're the ones who kidnapped Zoey?"

"We think so. We can't be sure, not 100 percent, but it looks like it."

"Why?" Tabitha hung her head, biting her lip. "And why give me one of their babies?"

"Well, that's the million-dollar question," Tad said. "Nobody really understands why the Fae exchange children. I don't think anybody has ever had the chance to ask them, and there's no guarantee we'd get a straight answer.

The Fae are scheming. Though I think, if the Zoey-replicant is a Woodling, she's not likely to be dangerous to you."

"Now that we have proof on film, we should bring the police into it. Millie knows me, she'll take this seriously." I pulled out my phone and searched through my contacts till I found her name. "I'm going to give her a call."

As Tad and Tabitha continued to speak, I moved to one side. Millie came on the line after two rings.

"Hey, Millie, it's January. We have a bit of a problem here—one you're already somewhat familiar with. Do you remember Tabitha Sweet coming to see you?"

"Oh, yeah," Millie said, sounding hesitant. "I have to tell you, I think she's a little loose in the nuts and bolts department."

"Time to think again, Millie. My office is investigating this case, and we just caught proof on tape that her baby really *isn't* Zoey. We're dealing with a changeling here. That child belongs to the Woodlings."

Millie was silent for a moment, then she let out a long sigh. "Oh lordy, that's even worse. What happened?"

I told her everything, starting from the first meeting Ari and I had with Tabitha. "It's an illusion so flawless that it's fooled the doctors. Fae glamour is nothing to muck around with. But it means that Zoey is actually missing, and she's probably with the Woodlings."

Millie dropped her voice. "January, do you know how many changeling cases are ever solved?"

"Few, from what I understand."

"Right. Making a trip into the Mystic Wood to confront the Woodlings is problematic and dangerous. That is, if you can find them in the first place.

Confronting any member of the Fae race is dangerous. We can't contain them in the jails, and believe me, I've tried on a couple occasions. They *always* manage to escape. We can't force them to tell us the truth—though usually they *do* come up with some twisted story that's half-truth, half-lies. We can't do much of anything about the situation. Now, I'll try my best, of course, but please, don't get Tabitha's hopes up. I'll be over in half an hour."

She hung up and I stared at my phone. I was getting tired of situations we couldn't wrap up in a tidy bow. So many cases in the world of the paranormal were unsolvable, from shadow men, to land wights rooting deep into an area, to ghosts that couldn't be chased away.

I turned to find Caitlin staring at me.

I gave her a faint shake of the head. "Millie's coming over." I didn't want to say more in front of Tabitha. Even though Millie had warned me not to get her hopes up, I didn't want to dash them, either.

"Well, we'll see what she has to say." Caitlin glanced at the clock. "When will she be here? It's three-twenty now."

I frowned. "She said half an hour. I can't stay late, by the way. I am meeting Killian's sister tonight. Talk about stress on top of stress. I need to go home and change."

"That's fine," Tad said. "Take off on the dot of five."

Hank and Tad were searching through the footage, looking for anything to give us any more information. Tabitha was lying down in her room, feeling faint. Caitlin and I headed into the kitchen to make a pot of tea for everyone.

"So, this has escalated rapidly," I said. "Ari and I would have been in way over our heads. I don't know what made us think we could take care of this on our own."

"Oh, I think you would have figured things out. It just might have taken longer. It's the same thing that makes us —as a group—think we can manage anything. The damage never seems quite as bad as it actually is until you get inside to survey the situation." She added, "I'm going to talk to my parents and tell them I'm not marrying Arlo. Talk about big implosions. I don't mind admitting that I'm nervous."

"As I said, you can always crash at my place. For what it's worth, I think you're doing the right thing, Caitlin. You can't marry a man you're not in love with, especially since your Pride doesn't encourage or approve of divorce. And you'd be doing him a disservice too. You both deserve someone who loves you as much as you love them." I glanced over at Tad, then back at her, holding her gaze.

She blushed, but ducked her head. "Thank you for the support. I appreciate it. I don't have many girlfriends I can talk to. Most of the girls I went to school with are married and totally absorbed in their families." She paused as the door to the nursery opened and Dr. Fairsight came back out.

I stood up. "Tabitha is lying down, Doctor. What did you find out?"

The doctor sat down on the sofa and motioned for us to join her. "To all outward appearances, that's a healthy little human girl. But I used an energy spectrogram, and a Fullon's species detector, and beneath the glamour, the energy indicates that yes, she's full-blooded Woodling. Now, without those tests, her bloodwork and everything else will show as human, but she's a changeling, all right."

I caught my breath. "Why do they do this?"

"Other than other humans, Woodlings are the worst offenders when it comes to kidnapping human children. Nobody knows why, but we speculate that it's because they have an extremely low birthrate, and a high infant mortality rate. So it's a rare event when a baby is born. They also live in a dangerous world with a number of natural predators and so we think they're trying to protect their children by hiding them away till they grow up. The easiest way is to trade them out for human babies. They raise those children as slaves, although from what I gather, they treat them well. But they're still slaves, and if a human child dies, it's not a tragedy for the race. If one of their own dies—it's a blow to their numbers."

I sighed. "Well, hell. So what do we do? How do we get Zoey back?"

"Normally, I'd think that the mother of this baby is raising Zoey. But since you saw her checking on her own child, I don't know. I'd guess that she's making certain that Ms. Sweet is taking care of the child. When you saw her, she ran to avoid capture." Dr. Fairsight shook her head. "As to finding Zoey, that's going to require a trip into the Mystic Wood, and then a lot of luck to find their territory."

I turned to Tad. "What do you know about this? Are the Woodlings dangerous? If I go stomping around in the forest, will they try to kill me?"

"Not likely, I *think*. There are Fae that are deadly, but I've never heard of the Woodlings outwardly attacking anyone, but that doesn't mean it hasn't happened. Oh, they would defend themselves if you threatened one of them, and they would go after you if you threaten their children, but I doubt if they'll do more than try to throw you off path—" Tad paused as Dr. Fairsight raised her hand.

"There are some cases where the Woodlings used other creatures to defend themselves. Like wolves, bears, mountain lions. So don't count on a lack of resistance. They just might not be the ones launching the arrows. Their defense is—like their minds—calculating and clever."

I sighed. "Well, what can we do? Obviously we can't leave Zoey out there. We have to at least try to find her. Even though Tabitha was concerned for little...whatever her name is, the baby in the crib, I doubt if she'll ever be able to love her or forget Zoey."

The doorbell rang again and I glanced at my watch. "That's probably Millie."

Hank answered the door. Sure enough, Millie entered the room, in uniform, her hair up in a messy bun. She looked tired and hassled.

"You okay?" I asked.

Millie shrugged. "I just finished booking a pervert who was slinking around a woman's house. He gave me a run for my money, but I managed to catch him. That will teach him to make sure he's wearing a belt. His pants fell down to his ankles and tripped him up."

I snorted, but quickly stopped at her look. She didn't look like she was in a joking mood.

"Ugh," I said. "Well, we have some news for you. Please, sit down." I motioned to Caitlin. "Can you get...the Zoey-wannabe, please?"

As Caitlin carried Zoey out to where we were sitting, Millie listened to our story. I introduced her to Dr. Fairsight, whom she already knew.

"So you are saying this really *isn't* Zoey?" Millie held up the snoozing baby and looked at her. "She looks so…normal."

"She has an incredibly strong glamour spell cast on her. One of the strongest I've come across. I would also hazard a guess that, since the mother knows you're aware of what's going on, there's a good chance she's going to try to rescue her baby. But she probably won't bring Zoey back. She'll leave some payment in the baby's place. The Fae don't steal, not outright, but my guess is she won't be able to free Zoey from where she's being held." Dr. Fairsight leaned back, crossing her legs as she eyed the Woodling child.

"I thought I'd go out in the wood, looking." Esmara might be able to help me, I figured. I wanted to take Ari, too, and I thought Killian would be a good choice to tag along. He might be able to sniff her out, given he was a wolf shifter. Whatever the case, as long as I didn't have to go alone, I'd be happy.

"What do you think the chances of my men finding the child if I send them in? That's a serious question, by the way. I don't want to make matters harder than they already are." Millie leaned forward, addressing the doctor.

"My guess is that that your men won't stand a chance in hell of finding her," Dr. Fairsight said. "No disrespect intended, but the moment the Woodlings sense authority coming into the Mystic Wood, they'll hide. You see, they're in violation of the treaty between the Fae and the human world. There's a no-kidnapping clause in there, because of the number of changelings that they've tried to substitute over the years. I'm thinking they don't want the government ripping out their woodlands and disrupting their ecosystem."

I frowned. "I've never heard of that before! You mean the Fae actually have a treaty worked out with the local government—"

"Not just the *local* government. No, we're talking on the federal level," Dr. Fairsight said. "The treaty was hammered out some years back. Honestly, very few people know about the existence of the Fae—oh, they hear bits and pieces, but it's like that rare tribe that gets mentioned in *National Geographic*, but people don't even realize they exist until they come across an obscure article. And the Fae aren't everywhere. They tend to stick to temperate climes where there are a lot of forests and woodlands. They aren't the same thing as nature spirits."

While this was all very interesting, I kept returning to the fact that Millie couldn't just go traipsing in there with her men, demanding the child back.

"And your testimony won't prove they've broken the treaty?" Caitlin asked.

Dr. Fairsight shook her head. "No. While I can probably get some of the authorities to accept my findings, at least on a theoretical level, that doesn't prove that the Fae left her as a changeling. And there are those in government who want to believe that they have the upper hand on all the Otherkin. Human men with massive greed who can't stand the thought that their power's not all-encompassing. They'll happily pretend that something doesn't exist rather than admit that they can't control everything. Plus..." She paused, letting out a sigh.

"What is it?" Tad asked.

"We have some suspicion that the Fae have bribed

certain officials so they'll overlook incidents like this. I've had two cases where a suspected changeling was involved. Both times, I testified to the court when the plaintiffs went after the Woodlings. Both times, the judge dismissed the cases *with prejudice*, saying there was no evidence to support the accusation. He threw out the evidence I provided. And both times, the judge in question had a sudden uptick in fortune. The first time, he bought a new convertible. I only noticed because I saw him riding around town in the car. A friend of mine who owns a luxury car dealership told me that Judge Jesop had paid cash for it. The second time, the judge—Jesop again—made a sizable donation to the Westward Research Foundation, where I do some work. That same week, research into the Woodlings and their way of life was cancelled, and instead the money was turned toward studies into shifter physiology."

"That doesn't prove the judge was on the take," Millie said. "But it's a strong coincidence."

"I can't prove that he took money from the Fae, but I notice these things. I doubt if a third attempt at proving the Woodlings stole a child would do any good." She sat back, frowning.

I glanced over at Tad. "Then, if we're going to retrieve Zoey, I guess we have to do it ourselves." I glanced at the doctor. "How long did it take for you to take those cases to trial, Dr. Fairsight?"

"Call me Linda, please. I have a feeling I'm going to be seeing more of you in the future," she added with a smile. "Anyway, to answer your question, it took us six weeks to secure a place on the docket."

"So those children were never found?" I asked.

She shook her head. "No, unfortunately. They weren't."

I had the feeling there was more to the story. "So, what happened to the families and the Woodling children? The changelings?"

Linda glanced around the room, her countenance darkening. "It's getting late. I'm sorry, but I have another appointment. Feel free to call me later and let me know how things are going. You have my number." And, without answering my question, she rose and headed to the door. As Hank saw her out, I glanced over at Millie, who was watching the doctor leave.

There's a reason Linda didn't want to talk in front of Millie, Esmara said. *Don't continue this discussion in front of your friend. I know you trust her, and she's not untrustworthy, but she took an oath and there are goings-on of which the authorities need to steer clear. And sometimes, it pays to be vague.*

Surprised by Esmara's statement but grateful for the advice, I turned to Millie. "Well, I guess we brought you out here for nothing. I'm sorry."

"No, that's all right," Millie said, looking concerned. "I wonder... I think I'll have a look into Judge Jesop's financials. Old Ivan—the judge—has run afoul of several groups who sought to have him disbarred, but each time, he managed to evade their accusations. I'll talk to you later. Call me if you need me." And she, too, left.

After she was gone, I told the others what Esmara had told me. "There's something Linda didn't want to tell us. I could feel it on the tip of her tongue, but Millie's presence made her stop."

"Well, she'll tell us if we need to know. Meanwhile, I suppose we're planning a trip into the forest," Tad said.

I stood, feeling torn. "I have to run. I need to change for dinner. I really can't be late tonight. Killian's counting on me to be there to meet his sister, and he's already half-convinced I don't want to meet his family."

Part of me felt like we shouldn't leave Tabitha alone now that she knew the truth, but the way she had comforted the Woodling child stuck in my mind. I didn't think she'd take it out on the baby.

"Go on, we'll finish up here. See you tomorrow morning. Eight on the dot." Tad waved me off.

I turned to Caitlin. "Remember, my offer is open."

She nodded. "I'll remember, thank you. If I end up needing to crash on your sofa, I'll call you."

"What's going on?" Tad asked.

Caitlin stared at the monitor, at the sleeping Woodling. "I'm telling my family that I won't go through with the arranged marriage. Arlo is pressing for a wedding date. So, I may be kicked out of my family and the Pride by tomorrow."

Tad's eyes shimmered for a moment, and I could see the wheels turning in his brain. But I didn't have time to stay.

"All right, I'll see you tomorrow. Somebody make sure Tabitha's all right before you leave." I slipped my jacket on.

As I headed out toward my car, I couldn't get my mind off the changeling. The poor baby, taken from its mother, set under a glamour that hid who she really was. It was bad enough to think of the human children, stolen away, but somehow, it seemed like the Zoey-imposter would also have a difficult future to face, as well as an identity crisis.

CHAPTER NINE

By the time I got home it was nearly five-thirty. I raced upstairs, yanking at my shirt. By the time I reached my bedroom, the shirt was off and I tossed it to the side, then pulled off my boots and shimmied out of my jeans. I rifled through the closet, finding a black halter dress with deep blue roses on it. It had a flowing skirt. I changed out for a strapless-look bra that had clear plastic straps, since strapless never worked well on G-cups, and then slid the dress over my head. I touched up my makeup and took my hair out of the ponytail, brushing it so the waves cascaded around my shoulders.

I added another coat of mascara, changed out my lip lacquer for a darker shade—a blackberry—and then slid on a black velvet blazer. I opted for a pair of moderate-heel pumps, also black velvet. I loved high heels, but they had to be chunky—I had long outgrown my stiletto days. In fact, I'd never been comfortable with spiked heels. Wearing a pair of Manolos set me up for a sprained ankle, given my unerring ability to find the only crack in an entire town of flat sidewalks. Finally, I sprayed a very light dusting of vanilla spice perfume on my wrists and tossed my phone, wallet, and keys into a black beaded clutch.

As I headed downstairs, the doorbell rang.

As I opened the door, there stood Killian and his sister, Tally. I could see the family resemblance. She was shorter, and had an athlete's body, but she had the same glow to her eyes, and the same curly light brown hair. She was also sporting a cane. Tally was dressed in a brown skirt and a green and orange paisley blouse, and her hair was held back by a matching scarf. She wore a camel-colored pea coat that was hanging open.

Killian introduced us then asked, "Do you want to head out? Our reservation is for six-twenty."

"Lucky's takes reservations?" I asked, surprised. Most diners didn't bother with reserving tables.

"Yeah, for dinner. They're a popular spot. So, are you ready?"

I nodded. "I have everything I need." I hadn't fed the cats, but then I usually fed them their second meal right before bedtime. Leaving the living room light on for them, and the porch light for me, I followed Killian and Tally out to his SUV. Tally was having some problems with her walking still, so I suggested she ride shotgun and I would sit in the back.

She gave me a grateful look. "Thank you. That would make it a lot easier for me to get in and out of the car."

Killian helped her in, then stopped me before I climbed into the back seat. "Thank you," he whispered. "That was really considerate."

"She's obviously still having problems from the accident," I said. "I'm not going to make things more difficult for her." I kissed him, then slid into the back seat and fastened my seat belt.

The trip down to the restaurant was pleasant enough. Tally seemed fairly easygoing, and she was talkative so that it didn't feel like I had to force the conversation.

"So, my brother tells me that you're witchblood?"

I nodded, then realized she couldn't see me from the front seat. "Yes, I am. My family was one of the founding families in Moonshadow Bay. We arrived here in the early 1900s."

"Our Pack originated in California, but during the big fires a few years ago, our lands were devastated. Instead of rebuilding, we decided to set out and join other packs. The Alpha had been killed during the fire, so we were minus a leader, and his widow didn't have the heart to take over until she could find a new mate." Tally cleared her throat. "It took another fire to get goofus here to join us." She poked her brother in the arm.

I blinked. I hadn't known any of that. Killian never seemed to be interested in discussing matters surrounding his Pack.

"Well, I'm glad he moved up here." I paused, then asked, "What made you choose the area you live in—Killian said you live near Mount Rainier, right?"

She nodded. "We live in Carbonado. We love the woods, and when my parents chose to move, I was living at home, after my divorce. They found a house right outside the town. I own a trailer home a little farther out. I work at the Carbonado Market. I'm a cashier."

I realized that I hadn't really asked Killian much about his family, although I knew bits and pieces. Feeling like I had maybe shortchanged him by ignoring that side of his life, I said, "So, what do your parents do? And your brother?"

"Darryn is living in Puyallup now. He's a mechanic. Our mother teaches fifth grade, and our father is an accountant." Tally paused, then said, "Killian said you were married before? I was too, which was a big mistake."

I remembered that Killian had mentioned—shortly after we first met—that Tally had been in a bad marriage. "Yeah, it was a mistake on my part too. He gaslighted me a lot, then cheated me out of a business that we built together. But that's done and over with."

"Sometimes things work out in ways you don't expect them to," Tally said. "I'm sorry you had to put up with that. My ex used to beat me whenever he got drunk, and he was an alcoholic."

"I still wish you'd let me go after him," Killian said in a low growl.

"I told you, no. I don't want you in trouble because I *know* you. He'd be dead and you'd be in prison. You do *not* have my permission to take him on. Besides, his liver will do the job for him. He's so far gone, I don't think he could stop if he wanted to."

We arrived at the restaurant. I popped out of the back seat and opened Tally's door, helping her out. She thanked me with a smile, and we filed into the diner. They had reserved a back booth for us and we slid in, Tally sitting on the outside where it was easiest for her to get in and out. Killian was sitting in the middle—it was a U-shaped booth—and I sat opposite Tally.

We ordered—fried chicken all around, and steak fries.

I asked for a chocolate milkshake, Killian wanted strawberry, and Tally asked for a root beer float.

"I love diner food," she said. "It's always so good. I'm a *Twin Peaks* fan—loved that show—and every time I go to a diner I want cherry pie."

I laughed. "I've watched reruns of the show and yeah, it does make cherry pie and coffee sound like the best thing in the world."

As we ate, we discussed my work. I told them about Tabitha and the Woodlings. "We're going to have to go into the Mystic Wood to see if we can track down Zoey. I'm not looking forward to tangling with the Woodlings. I saw one last night. Killian was with us."

"Yes, I was, and the thought of you heading into the woodland to try to find the kid doesn't sit well with me. I'll come with you. You're not equipped to fight back if they get rough. And from what I understand, some of the Fae can play *very* roughly."

I nodded. "Yeah, I understand that as well. The Woodlings aren't like the Tuatha de Dannan, but they're devious. They also remind me of sculptures."

"They're only nominally humanoid, and who knows if that's even their normal shape," Killian said.

"Well, whatever the case, I'm not optimistic about finding Zoey." I sighed, picking at my chicken.

"Eat up," Killian said. "There's nothing you can do tonight to help." He paused. "By the way, have you had any chance to look over the things you found from your great-grandmother?"

Relieved at the change in subject, I nodded. "Yes, actually. I found her book of shadows—it's a magical diary, so to speak. And I've started reading it. I haven't got very far, but I thought I might tackle some more this evening."

"You found your great-grandmother's diary?" Tally asked. "That would be fascinating. I don't think we ever met our great-grandmother," she added. "Have we?"

Killian shook his head. "She died before we were born." He turned to me. "Great-Grandma Ina was shot by a hunter while she was in her alt-form. He was charged with murder—the court managed to prove that he knew who she was and that she was going into the woods in her wolf form, and it was well known that he hated shifters. When they cross-examined him, he broke down on the stand and confessed. The court turned him over to the Pack for justice. He was sentenced to work for Great-Grandpa for twenty years, and if he tried to run off, he'd be hanged. He put in a lot of years and from what I understand, he ended up trying to make up for what he did, once he saw how it affected the family."

"I guess some people can change," I said, though it was hard for me to believe.

"Some, but I never count on it," Killian said.

I turned to Tally. "How's your leg doing? You were pretty broken up there, from what Killian was telling me."

"I'm healing, but I may never be the same. Now that I can take my alt-shape again, it's a bit better—I do much better in wolf form, to be honest. I don't hurt as much, I can move better. Sometimes, I take my alt-form for the night because I sleep better that way."

It suddenly occurred to me what a different world they lived in. They had two sides to their life, literally. I'd never really thought too much about being anything other than a witch, but now I wondered what it was like to be a shifter.

"It must be so cool to be able to change shape," I said. "You have two completely different worlds you live in."

"Hey, I was just thinking it must be really fun to be able to work with magic. I admit, it scares me, and I shy away from it," Tally said. "But I still think it's cool. I guess the grass always does seem greener."

She paused as Killian excused himself to go to the restroom. While he was gone, she said, "You do realize that he's nuts over you? I like you, January. I like you a lot. I came prepared to pick you over and find any problems I could because you're witchblood and not Pack. But…I like you. However, I want you to know, my big brother is one of the dearest people in my life. Don't toy with his heart. Don't hurt him. He's far more sensitive than you might think."

I had expected the "Don't hurt my brother" speech to be trotted out, because that would be exactly something I would do, so I wasn't offended.

"I won't. I care about your brother…" I paused, blushing. It was getting harder and harder not to use the "L" word.

But Tally caught it. She broke out in a wide smile. "You love him, don't you?"

I started to shake my head, but then stopped. "I haven't said anything yet. Please don't tell him. I need to do so in my own way, when I'm sure of his feelings."

She paused, then glanced toward the restrooms. "One thing you should know about Pack. Once we've chosen a mate, we're done. We date, we go out, but there's a point where we know. And my brother… He's chosen a mate. I can tell. So don't feel you have to wait too long."

At that moment, Killian appeared from the men's room door, and Tally changed the subject. I sat there, listening to her talk, thinking about what she said. Was she right? Did Killian love me? Had he decided I was his mate? And was I even ready for that? With all those questions rumbling around in my brain, I turned the subject toward dessert, and tried to focus on the evening at hand.

THAT NIGHT, I CALLED ARI TO FILL HER IN ON WHAT WAS going on, but that conversation was cut short when she burst into tears upon hearing my voice.

"What's wrong? Are you okay?"

"Meagan's mother came to see me today. She told me to break the engagement or she'll ruin my business." Ari was sobbing like I'd never heard her cry.

"What the hell? What kind of asshole is she?"

"She's… You know how Meagan told you her family acted when she came out?"

"Yeah, I remember."

Meagan's mother had been furious, insisting that Meagan return to her husband because he "was a good catch" and she was "shaming the family." While most bear shifter clans tended to be matriarchal, they didn't all approve of same-sex marriages. Family lineage was important, and having blood-children was extremely important in their society.

"Well, her mother blames *me* for Meagan 'turning gay' and she threatened to ruin my business if I don't break off the engagement. I knew they were pissed at her, but I can't believe they would do this. Her mother is pretty high up in social circles. She could spread the word and I'd lose half my customers."

"What did Meagan say?"

Ari sniffled. "I haven't told her yet. I was just going to call you—Mrs. Lopez just left a few minutes ago." Meagan had gone back to her maiden name when she left her ex.

"You need to tell her. Meagan *has* to talk to her mother." I felt helpless. I wanted to run over to the Lopez house and beat some sense into the woman, but running afoul of a bear shifter wasn't exactly the best tactic to take.

"How can I? Meagan's just been getting back on an even keel with her parents. This is going to either break us up, or sever her ties with them. There's no way Mrs. Lopez will come around."

I sighed. Everybody seemed to be having family troubles. "Listen, *you* talk to Meagan or I will. She needs to know what her mother is up to. You're her fiancée. She's the love of your life. Don't let this happen without a fight. And if old lady Lopez tries to ruin your business, we'll just make sure people know *why*. I've got a big mouth when I choose to use it."

Ari laughed at that. "So, how did the big dinner go?"

"Actually, better than I thought. Tally's nice. I found out more about Killian's family." I paused, then added, "Tally told me that Killian's in love with me. She gave me *the* speech. You know the one."

" 'Don't hurt my brother'?"

"Essentially. But I like her. I was afraid, at first, because I had such a bad run-in with Ellison's parents."

But at least they didn't threaten to ruin you if you married him, a little voice whispered, and I had to admit, that was true. Granted, they treated me like I was pond scum, but they didn't threaten my livelihood.

"So, what's Killian's sister like?"

I told Ari about her. "The accident messed her up pretty good, and I feel bad for her. She looks like she was athletic, but now she's having trouble walking without a cane. I hope she sues the hell out of that driver. He was speeding—there was no doubt about that, given the skid marks he left when he tried to swerve. Cops pegged him as going at least sixty-five miles an hour on a forty-mph stretch of road."

"She was in her alt-shape, wasn't she?"

"Yeah, and when the car hit her, it threw her thirty feet to the side. If she was human, she would have died." I paused, then added, "Talk to Meagan."

Ari let out another sigh. "She worked late tonight. She should be getting home any second. I'll tell her when she gets here, I promise." She hesitated, then said, "You don't think she'll leave me, do you?"

"I don't think so. If she ditched her ex because she knew she was gay, and came out to her parents knowing the way they'd react, she's not going to throw you over because of her mother. It seems to me that Meagan has already made her choice, and you're it."

I hung up, hoping to hell I was right. If I wasn't, there would be a lot of pieces to pick up.

THE NEXT MORNING, XI WOKE ME UP EARLY. SHE BATTED my face until I opened my eyes and stared at the little fluff ball.

"What? What do you want?" I muttered, patting her head.

She mewed and patted at my nose again. Then she mewed a second time and bounced off the bed, racing over to the window. Groggy, I shoved my way out from beneath the covers and followed her.

There, in the backyard, something was glittering on the lawn. It was small, I couldn't make out what it was from the second floor, but I definitely saw it. There was something else that caught my eye—the bushes near the tree line were rustling.

Frowning, I leaned down and scooped up Xi, holding her up to stare in her eyes. "What did you see out there? What is it, baby?"

She let out a mew and connected with me, and I caught a sudden glimpse of a strange creature, looking very much like a Woodling, prowling in my backyard.

"Was there a Woodling out there?" I asked.

Xi mewed again. I kissed her nose, then set her on the writing desk beneath the window so she could stare outside. As I quickly dressed, sliding on jeans and a sweater, then quickly jamming socks on my feet and sliding on my ankle boots, Xi continued to make little chattering sounds as she stared out the window. I knew that cats did that when they saw birds, but this was different. She was talking about something out there, I just couldn't catch the drift of her conversation. Familiars weren't talkative like you saw on TV, but they could—and did—communicate. But Xi was very young and it would take her time to reach that stage. For now, it was vague impressions and images.

I pulled my hair back in a quick ponytail and headed downstairs. It was six A.M., so I had some time before work. I stepped onto the back porch, making sure the door wasn't locked before I closed it behind me. As I clattered down the steps, the entire yard felt lit up with energy. Sure enough, something had been out there.

I followed the path through the center of the grass until I came to the object I had seen from my window. I picked it up, carefully examining it. The contraption was made of a gold-tone metal, and it reminded me of a carousel, only with crystal unicorns instead of horses on it. As I held it up, I saw a knob beneath the thing, along with four furrows into the metal. I wound the knob like you wind a watch, and the unicorns began to rotate. The sight was mesmerizing as rainbows filtered through the crystal unicorns, reflecting out to sparkle in the early morning gloom.

I caught my breath, entranced. Then, suddenly wary, I gazed at the tree line and the path leading into the wood. A Woodling had brought this to me, and there had to be some reason. Then a thought hit me. What if the mother of the Woodling child had brought this to me to give to her baby?

Frowning, I reached out to see if Esmara was nearby. *Is this enchanted? Is it cursed, hexed, or bewitched?*

No, Esmara said. *It's not cursed. But neither is it made by human hands. It's very old. I know what you're thinking, and you may be right—but I cannot tell. But it's safe to have in your house.*

Thank you. I was wondering whether to take it inside. I glanced back at the woodland. The Mystic Wood surrounded the town on three sides. It wouldn't be that much of a stretch for the Woodling mother to have found me.

I carried it inside, wishing I could call my grandmother. Rowan Firesong would be a huge help at this point, but she was off on a road trip and she hadn't told me where she was going. I could text her, but she had been explicit about not bothering her unless it was life or death, and I didn't think she'd consider this situation fitting into that category.

I examined the carousel closely. There were no batteries from what I could see, which meant it operated from the winding key. It was beautifully made, all crystal and gold, and shimmering. As I sat down at the kitchen table, I couldn't keep my eyes off of it.

Xi shook me out of my fascination, leaping on the table and mewing for breakfast. Klaus joined her. Startled, I pushed the carousel back to where the cats couldn't knock it off, and proceeded to feed them.

"Well, little buggers, looks like the Woodlings are reaching out on their own," I told them as they ate. "At least, I *think* it's them—the mother, at least. I'll take this to work with me." As soon as they were chowing down on their food, I ran upstairs and tidied up, put on my makeup, then brushed my hair back into a tidier ponytail and draped a scarf around my neck that matched the sweater.

It was time for work, and I was ready to go. Gathering up the carousel, I headed for the door, stopping only to text Ari to ask how her talk with Meagan went. By the time I started my car, she hadn't answered, so I figured she was busy with an appointment.

CHAPTER TEN

*A*ri still hadn't answered by the time I got to work. I parked my car in front of the office, picked up the carousel, and headed inside. I waved to Wren, who was on the phone, and slipped behind the desk to the door leading to the inner office.

Caitlin was settling in at her desk, Hank was already glued to the bank of monitors, and Tad was sitting on the edge of his desk, frowning over what looked like a letter—as in an actual *letter*, not an email.

"Well, look what someone left me this morning," I said, setting the carousel down on the table that we gathered around for meetings. "My gut tells me the Woodling mother left this in my backyard for me to give to her baby. It's magical, but not cursed—Esmara confirmed that. I'm now thinking that the mother Woodling didn't want to give up her baby. I wonder if she had a choice. What do we know about their society?"

"Not much," Tad said, setting the letter down and walking over to look at the carousel. "That's beautiful." He picked it up and examined it. Hank and Caitlin joined us. "What makes you think it's from a Woodling?"

"Xi shot me an image of it."

Tad jerked his head up. "Xi, as in Xi your kitten?"

"Yes, *that* Xi. She's growing into a familiar, so we have a bond. Familiars, regardless of their form, aren't just regular animals. They're guides—similar to spirit guides, only in animal form. They have an expanded capacity for reason and the ability to communicate with the witch they're bonded to."

"All right, so she saw a Woodling in your yard, then?"

"Right, and she woke me up to tell me about it. I looked out the window and saw something glittering in the middle of the yard. I went outside to see what it was, and Esmara told me that it wasn't made by human hands." I glanced over at the console at the coffeepot and saw that it was empty. "No java juice?" I frowned. "I need caffeine to function, guys, you know that."

"You almost always bring your own. Hank finished the last of it, he should be the one to make a new pot," Caitlin said, pointing her finger at him and grinning.

"Tattletale," Hank muttered. "Tell you what, I know you're hardcore and prefer espresso. I'll run over to the coffee shop, since I want a mocha. Even the three cups that I drank wasn't enough to get me moving today. I had a long night."

"What happened?" Tad asked, his eyes narrowing. "You all right?"

"I'm fine, but my mother isn't," Hank replied. "I got a call from my father last night. Mom broke her leg. They were hiking up in the Cascades and a rock under her foot slipped. She tried to catch herself but ended up sliding down the rockface. She reached out with her feet to slow the fall—she was fastened to a belay rope, but Dad wasn't fast enough. One of her feet got caught in a crack and it twisted her as she continued to fall. Dad managed to brace her, but by then her leg was torqued in a 90-degree angle. She has three breaks in the leg. She's not going climbing anytime soon."

"Your *parents* are rock climbers?" I asked. It was hard to imagine. Hank wasn't as young as he looked—he was also witchblood and he had lived for quite a while.

"Yeah, they enjoy it. They've climbed all the big peaks, except for Everest. They want to try for the summit but I keep talking them out of it. They're in that stage of life where their sense of adventure outweighs their physical abilities and their common sense. It's almost harder to slow down when you've always been super athletic." He shrugged. "Anyway, she's stuck in the hospital for a week before they move her to a rehab center to help her with her knee. Dad called at one A.M. That's when the search and rescue team found them."

"You definitely need the caffeine," I said. "You want me to go?"

He yawned, shaking his head. "The cool air will wake me up. Orders all around?"

I asked for a triple-shot caramel latte and Caitlin wanted a chai tea. Tad asked for an extra-large coffee with four sugars in it, handing Hank the company credit card as he did so.

"It's hard to imagine him having parents, let alone parents who are out climbing mountains," I said. "I don't know much about his background."

"His family has some pretty potent witchblood in it,

but Hank's family was never around much when he was growing up, from what I understand. He was brought up by a nanny, who was all business. Not abusive, mind you, but she wasn't the type to coddle her charges." Caitlin glanced at the carousel. "What are you going to do with that?"

"I thought I might take it over to Tabitha's later on. Meanwhile, what are we going to do about the Woodlings? And what was Dr. Fairsight hiding last night?"

My phone jangled and I glanced at the text. It was from Ari.

MEAGAN WANTS TO POSTPONE THE WEDDING. WE HAD A HUGE FIGHT AND SHE STORMED OUT. JANUARY, WHAT AM I GOING TO DO?

"Oh crap," I muttered. I glanced over at Tad, wondering if I could talk my way out for the day. But he was once again looking at the letter he had been holding, and by the expression on his face, he wasn't overjoyed at the news.

"January, I have a job for you," he said, just as I was about to ask for the rest of the day off. "I was wondering if you'd take care of this for me?" He handed me the letter.

I glanced at the page. It was a letter asking for a speaker to give a lecture at the local school about crypto-zoology in early April. "I'm not qualified to do this," I said. "I may be Otherkin—but I'm not an expert by any means. And I've only been working here since December. What about giving this to Hank or Caitlin?"

Tad frowned. "I tried. Neither of them wanted to do it."

"Well, I'm not going to do a very good job, and I guarantee you those kids are going to ask far more questions than I'm able to answer."

Tad let out an exasperated sigh. "Fine. I'll do it." He grabbed the letter back out and tossed it on his desk. "Where the hell is Hank? We need to get started on the morning meeting."

I knew that we had nothing pressing, so his irritation had to be coming from somewhere else. I glanced over at Caitlin, who was studiously staring at the wall. The tension in the room was thick, and it dawned on me that there was an undertone between the pair of them that was subtle but thick. Either Tad had said something to Caitlin or vice versa and whatever the subject was, it hadn't gone over well. Now was not the time to ask for the day off.

I decided to try to break the tension. "I met Killian's sister last night."

Caitlin immediately latched onto my words. "That's right, you did. How did it go? What's she like?"

Tad did the same. "Do you get along with her? She was in an accident recently, wasn't she?"

I brought out every detail I could remember of the dinner, trying to muster up as much enthusiasm as I could over the evening. While it had gone well, it hadn't been quite as bright and sparkly as I made it out to be. But the ploy worked, and by the time Hank returned with our coffee, Caitlin and Tad were both smiling again.

"All right, let's start this meeting," Tad said. "I'll get my files."

I settled in at the round table and took the opportunity to text Ari. I WISH I COULD GET FREE AND COME OVER BUT I DON'T THINK THAT'S GOING TO BE POSSIBLE FOR AT LEAST

THE MORNING. ARE YOU OKAY? IS THERE ANYTHING I
CAN DO?

NOT UNLESS YOU CAN CONVINCE HER MOTHER TO QUIT
ACTING LIKE AN ASSHOLE. CALL ME WHEN YOU CAN. I'M
GOING TO GO FOR A RUN. I CANCELLED MY APPOINTMENTS
THIS MORNING.

I stared at my phone, wishing I could do more. I knew
that talking to Meagan's mother would do no good, but
maybe I could talk to Meagan and try to help her see
reason. I quickly searched through my contacts to find
Meagan's number and texted her. She wasn't answering,
so I asked her to get in touch with me.

"Excuse me, January? If you'd care to give us your
attention?" Tad's voice broke through my thoughts.

Startled, I looked up to see all four of my coworkers
staring at me. "Sorry, I have an urgent matter that I'm
kind of involved in."

"Work-related?"

I shook my head. "No, personal."

"Is it an emergency?" Tad asked. I could tell he was
enjoying this little cat and mouse game.

"Not in the truest sense of the word."

"Then perhaps you'd care to join the discussion?"

I sighed. "Sorry, but this really is difficult. Meagan
wants to postpone the wedding because her mother is
threatening Ari's reputation if they go through with it."

That wiped the smirk off Tad's face. He sat down,
frowning. "What the hell?"

"Meagan's mother has always been upset that Meagan
came out of the closet, and she was even more upset that
Meagan left what was seen as a fortuitous marriage. Now,
she's blaming Ari for everything and has threatened to

destroy her business if they go through with their wedding." I shrugged. "And I'm sitting here watching things fall apart."

"I'm sorry," Tad said, contritely. "I didn't realize it was so serious."

"There's not much I can do, but I'm thinking if I can talk to Meagan and find out why she's caving into her mother's demands, maybe I can help. But she won't answer my texts, or she can't just yet. I hope it's the latter, not the former."

"Well, we're just all having a day, aren't we?" Caitlin said. "Can we just get on with business? The sooner this day is over, the happier I'll be."

Tad paused, looking around the table. "All right, listen up. We've all been working hard, and doing a great job. Yes, we have to go searching in the Mystic Wood for the Woodlings, but that's not going to happen today and I think we all know that. For one thing, if you want Killian to come along with us, then he needs to be here. January, if you can ask him when he'll be able to join us? Other than that, the hunt for bigfoot's going to take time, since we have so many sightings to sort through. For those reasons, I'm declaring today a holiday. Go. Take care of the things you need to take care of. Be free, my children." He waved his arms like a bird and squawked, producing a laugh from all of us.

As we gathered up our things, I sidled over to Caitlin. "What's going on?"

"You want to stop in at Lucky's and talk over pie?" she asked.

"Do you mind if I ask Ari to join us?"

"Ask away." She slid into her coat and gathered her

things as I did the same. The carousel, I left in the office. It seemed the safest place for it.

As we headed out the door, I texted for Ari to meet Caitlin and me at Lucky's and she said she'd be there in fifteen minutes. Overhead, the sky was weeping, gray and overcast with spring rain. A light wind was blowing, and I couldn't help but feel that change was in the air.

LUCKY'S WAS JUMPING, BUT WE MANAGED TO FIND A BOOTH near one of the wide windows. We were about to order pie when I decided that I hadn't eaten enough for breakfast, so I ordered a bowl of chicken soup and a roll to go with the pie. Caitlin ordered a side of fries.

Ari showed up a few moments later. She hustled over and slid in beside Caitlin so she could face me, and pulled off her gloves and slid out of her jacket. She was wearing sunglasses, though, and when I motioned for her to take them off, her eyes were red and teary and her nose looked puffy.

"Oh, Ari, I'm so sorry." I reached across the table to take her hands. "Why does she want to postpone the wedding?"

"I think she's afraid her mother will make good on her threats and Meagan's trying to protect my business. But I don't want her to do that—she shouldn't sacrifice our happiness because of one old biddy's bigotry. Granted that old biddy is her mother, but hey, if the label fits, wear it. What drives me nutty is that Mrs. Lopez is constantly saying, *Oh I have a gay friend,* or *Well, my daughter is gay so I know all about the issues…* You know the type."

I nodded. "Bigotry is alive and well and crosses all boundaries." I turned to Caitlin. "How about you? Did you tell your parents you aren't marrying Arlo?"

She nodded. "Why do you think I was so off this morning?"

Ari frowned. "What's going on? I'd like to think about somebody else's problems other than mine for a while."

"Last night, I told my parents that I'm not going through with the arranged marriage. We've been engaged for years—since I was young—but even though I know him and have grown up around him, I don't love him. When I think about spending my future with him, no future at all sounds better." She shifted in her seat. I could tell that it had not gone well.

"So, what did they say?" I asked. "Do you need to stay on my sofa?"

"Thanks, but I'm staying with a friend until I find an apartment. I'll be out of the dorms by tonight. My mother and father yelled at me for two solid hours. I'm disgracing the family name and their reputation will be ruined and they won't be able to face their friends, and on and on. Not once did they say a single word that indicates they care anything about my own happiness. My father is frantic that he'll have to pay a severance dowry—if a bride refuses to marry, sometimes her father is forced to pay a substantial loss fee to the family of the groom."

"Cripes, it's like a kill fee in writing. But you're a person, not a short story or a novel."

"In my Pride, I belong to my parents until I either marry or leave the Pride. Which is why most women go through with the marriages even if they don't want to. "So now I have two choices. I have twenty-four hours to tell my parents I'll relent and marry Arlo, or they'll record the decision in the Pride Roll Book and I will be *casta*—an outcast. I'll be on my own, for good."

She sounded so desolate that I wanted to hug her. Ari did, since she was sitting next to her. "That's awful. There's no provision for those who want to remain single?"

Caitlin shrugged. "There are some women who are autonomous. If you're widowed, you don't have to remarry. If your parents can't make you a match, you can be designated a 'woman of independent means' as long as your father gives you enough money to start out on. But if you do decide to marry after that, it has to be approved by your parents if they're still living, or the Elders, if your parents are dead. Even if you're sixty freaking years old, you have to abide by their decision. If they disapprove of your choice, then you can either break up and stay part of the Pride, or you can walk away and, once again, become casta. Women can work, as long as they do their duty to the Pride and marry and at least attempt to bear children."

"Your Pride sounds stuck in the 1800s."

"My Pride is stuck in the *dinosaur* era. Anyway, I can't relent. I can't marry Arlo. Once I made my decision, I was so relieved that I know it's the right choice. I'd be miserable and I wouldn't make him happy. For the rest of his life, he'd know he had a wife who was just going through the motions. And we'd both end up bitter and angry. I've seen it before." She paused as the waitress arrived with our food. After taking Ari's order, she left us alone.

"Your people are harsh," Ari said. "But then, so are a lot of people in the world."

"They cling to patterns from days when we needed to

grow our population, to keep the Pride from dying out. But those days are gone. There are enough of us, and yet the Elders hold onto their power like it's gold." Caitlin nibbled on a fry.

I began eating my soup. "What was going on with Tad? I sensed something beneath the surface."

"You're right. When I got to work, I told him all about what happened. He started thumping his chest about how he'd talk to my parents for me, and all that. I've never seen him so…*testosteroney*, if you know what I mean. I told him I'd handle it and I think I hurt his ego. Well, I know I did. I told him that if I wanted his help, I'd ask for it. That it wasn't his place."

I blushed, thinking of my text to Meagan and wondering if I'd overstepped the line. "Um, he just wanted to help, but yeah…" I glanced at Ari. "So, has Meagan texted you?"

"No, and she's letting all messages go to voice mail. I know she tends to withdraw when she's in a confrontation—well, usually. She didn't when she finally broke it off with her ex-husband. But Meagan is so disappointed in her mother that I have no clue what she's up to now. I'm worried about her. I texted her to just let me know if she's okay, but she hasn't sent me a single message."

Ari looked so worried that I wanted to throttle Meagan. Storming out after an argument was one thing, but keeping your partner worried was downright rude and hurtful.

"Maybe she's driving and can't answer," I said.

"And maybe I'm not really pissed," Ari said. But I could tell she was more concerned than angry.

We moved onto other subjects, with me trying to raise

both Caitlin's and Ari's spirits, but in the end, we just ate our way through an entire chocolate cream pie. But I didn't give a damn. I was there for my friends, and that was all that mattered. And if it took chocolate cream pie to take the edge off, so be it.

CHAPTER ELEVEN

*A*fter we finished our brunch, Ari took off to do some shopping for salon supplies, and Caitlin decided she needed to stop in at the spa for a massage. As much as I cared about them, I was grateful because I couldn't think of anything else to try to perk them up. I wanted to be there for them, I wanted to help, but I didn't have the knack for making people feel better.

I headed home, relieved to have the rest of the day to myself. As I hung up my jacket and kicked off my boots, I felt a sense of relief sweep over me. I looked around, feeling at peace. I really did finally feel like this was my home, my sanctuary.

When I was young it had always felt comfortable but temporary. Then when I moved away, it was my parents' home. And none of the apartments or houses I had shared with Ellison had truly felt like home, either. He had always had the final decision on everything.

But in the past two months, I had settled back into Moonshadow Bay and established a connection like I had never before managed. I was putting down roots. I no longer felt like I was searching for a place where I belonged. This was my home, and that sense of foundation felt good.

I padded to the kitchen in my socks. I used refillable plastic bottles that had no BPA in them, and just filled them and kept them in the fridge so that I always had ice-cold water. I added a squirt of sugar-free lemon flavoring to the bottle and shook it up, taking a long drink from it before I sat down at the table. There, I pulled Great-Grandma Colleen's book of shadows over to me and flipped it open to a random entry.

Colleen's Book of Shadows
  Entry: May 3, 1923

  We are broken. My beautiful Lara vanished and I know where she is, but Brian insists I'm wrong. I'm furious with him. Our daughter is gone, likely held prisoner, yet he listens to Rowan Firesong more than he listens to me. I've grown to hate that woman. She insinuates herself into our lives like a snake.

  Yesterday I asked Lara to gather together a basket of rolls and bread so I could take them to old Annie Morrow. Annie is near seventy, deaf as a stone post, and the biggest gossip in town. But she's also a witch in need and my mother taught me that we always look after our own when they need help. Indeed, we look after *all* our neighbors, for when we may be in need, their goodwill might be all we have to get us through the harder times. So I send Annie a basket of bread each week, and tuck a jar of jelly in with it and a few other tidbits I know she's fond of.

My dear Lara volunteered to make the journey. I didn't like her going through the forest alone, but by faith and magic, she insisted she could do it, and since I had no one else to watch Naomi, I agreed. I let her run off into the wild wood without a care.

She never came home. When twilight approached, I began to worry and I asked Brian to go look for her. The vampires come out after dark. He did so, and came home white as a ghost. He was carrying the basket—still filled with bread, though the jelly was gone, and there was my Lara's shawl with it.

All the men in Moonshadow Bay turned out for the search, but though they looked high and low, they could not find her. I trust they looked—they are good men, men with stout hearts and no end to courage. But not a hair of my Lara's head did they find. Just the basket of bread and shawl, on the inner borders of the magical woodland.

I told Brian that in my heart, I know she's not dead. I can still feel the connection—there's a strong bond between my Lara and me, and the only thing that can sever that is death. I want her home, to tend to her and to see her rest peacefully, yet I fear we'll go year after year, always wondering.

Rowan—and I curse her name—said that we should forget her. That if she was caught up by a Woodling there's no hope and she'll be trapped as a slave forever. In my heart, I fear she might be right, though I can't bring myself to believe it. As much as

I detest that woman, she's generally right about matters. She wears on me, she does, but she was very kindly this evening when she was here, and she paused by Lara's bed and looked at it.

"Best to use that for one of your other wee ones," Rowan said.

"You mean until she returns," said I.

"Colleen, you know what I mean," she said.

Brian tells me to accept the loss, that my instinct is off and that somehow our girl met a sudden end. But I still believe that my Lara will return safely to us. And even now, Brian is over at Rowan's place while he should be here in our home, in our bed comforting me. I lie here alone, under the covers, trying to soothe the other children. Trixie and Esmara know something's wrong, Prue's not sure what's going on, and Naomi's clueless, being the loving little lump she is. So I stay strong for them, even though inside, I am weeping.

I know the Woodlings stole my daughter. I know it in my heart and soul. And I won't rest until we find her and bring her home.

I stared at the entry, shaking my head. Unable to wait, I flipped through the entries, scanning quickly, until I came to one five days later, where I saw Lara's name in bold print.

Colleen's Book of Shadows
   Entry: May 8, 1923

And so, she was right. Rowan Firesong was right, my daughter is dead. I still can't believe this. I still can't accept it. I swear I can feel her alive. But the sheriff found her body down by the bay, half in, half out of the water. She drowned.

Brian was out chopping wood for the stove yesterday before he went into town when Rowan and the sheriff rode in. The sheriff was astride his horse, looking for all the world like a prince astride a white steed, with Rowan behind him. He passed by Brian, not noticing him, and knocked on the door. Little Trixie answered, though I told her no opening the door to strangers. But she did anyway and he asked to see me, and I came to the door and then I realized that yes, it was the sheriff visiting, and that made me terribly nervous.

I remember every nuance of his character. I remember the look on his face. It was shock and worry and tension and sadness. I asked him in, thinking Brian would notice he was here and join us, but Brian apparently was absorbed in his own thoughts and so I made certain the baby was in her crib, and that Prue, Trixie, and Esmara were off in their room, playing.

I offered Rowan and the sheriff some tea, because that's what you do, isn't it? You offer someone tea and a scone or a biscuit. So I did.

And they accepted the tea but said no to the pastry. I brought them a piping hot cuppa and we sat at the table. He looked uncomfortable and Rowan kept biting her lip, and I knew there was something wrong. I could feel it—could sense it like I can smell perfume.

And then they asked where Brian was, so I went to the door and called him in. And we all sat there with tea for a few minutes, with me awkwardly asking if anybody wanted sugar and cream. And finally, he just came out and said it. As clear as day. As clear as spun sugar.

"Ma'am, I'm sorry to tell you and the mister that I found your daughter Lara. She drowned, down by the edge of the bay."

And of course, I was screaming, and they had to lead me over to the rocking chair where I sat and rocked and cried as the sheriff told us what happened.

I recall him mentioning the water and me screaming because Lara loved the water and how could she die in something she loved? And then he told us that some pervert had done horrible things to her, things I'll never repeat but that will burn in my memory forever, and the rest of the afternoon is a blur.

Brian tells me they had to strap me down until Rowan gave me a sedative, some Wissel-Will, and I almost broke free of the restraints but they tightened them, and the sedative finally worked. Now it's the next morning, and my Lara is still dead, and I can never face life the same way again. And I swear, if I find out who took my daughter from me, I will rip out his heart while it's still beating, and eat it for lunch.

I SAT BACK, STARING GRIMLY AT THE PAGE. THE WORDS might be nearly a hundred years old, but the energy on the page was still palpable. I let out a long breath, realizing I'd been holding it as I read. So, my great-grandmother had believed that the Woodlings took Lara, but instead, the girl had been murdered. And brutally so, given the innuendos in Colleen's journal entry.

I pushed back the book of shadows, sitting back to think. The Woodlings were in the thicket even then—but that made sense. They tended to stay in warmer climes, in the forests. I wondered if, as the deforestation continued, they would fight back? Or would they fade away? Feeling uncountably sad, I made myself another mocha and glanced at the clock. It was nearly two. I was thinking about what to do with myself during the afternoon when my phone pinged.

CAN I COME OVER AND TALK TO YOU? The text was from Meagan.

Debating for a moment, I finally answered. YES, PLEASE DO. ARI'S WORRIED SICK ABOUT YOU.

I KNOW. I'D LIKE TO EXPLAIN. BUT PLEASE DON'T TELL HER THAT I CONTACTED YOU. NOT YET.

ALL RIGHT. BUT YOU'D BETTER HAVE A GOOD EXPLANATION.

Meagan showed up about fifteen minutes later. I led her into the living room. Bear shifters were usually quite athletic, and Meagan was no exception. She had been the star cheerleader in high school and one of the mean girls, but she had grown into a pleasant-tempered woman who did a top-notch job as a high school gym teacher. She was tall and muscled, with long legs and blond hair. She had even won a few powerlifting competitions in her Otherkin weight category. She coached girls' gymnastics, and was especially attentive to the problems facing gymnasts, like abusive private coaches, eating disorders, and pushing the body beyond what it was capable of.

"Sit down," I said, motioning for her toward the sofa. "Would you like something to drink?"

She shook her head. As she sat down, Klaus ran up and scrambled up her pants leg, then up her chest to lick her on the nose. She laughed, but I could tell she had been crying. Her eyes were red and puffy, and her makeup was blotched.

"Thanks, but no. I wanted to talk to you. I can't talk to Ari about this, not right now."

"So, your mother has threatened to destroy Ari's business if you marry her, have I got that right?"

Meagan nodded. "Yeah, she has. I told Ari to give me some time, that I could take care of it, but she's so freaked about my mother not supporting me that she won't listen. She's not angry about her business, she's angry on my behalf."

"Isn't that what's supposed to happen when you're engaged to someone?" I frowned, not understanding yet what had caused the rift.

"It's just… I talked to the leader of the Pride. He told me that if I petition the Elder Council to sever my ties to my family, then my mother won't be socially affected by what I choose to do and I could ask the Pride to intercede if she tried to destroy Ari's business. So I've filled out the application. But it's going to take a couple of months given the number of cases before the Elders right now. I didn't tell Ari that I wanted to postpone the wedding. I told her we should put any talk of it on hold—publicly. She misunderstood and blew up. I tried to calm her down, tried to tell her that everything would work out, but she won't listen."

I frowned, then asked, "So, you didn't tell her that you're petitioning for autonomy and that the reason you want to keep a lid on public discussion is to throw your mother off guard?"

Meagan paused, then, her eyes widening, she shook her head. "No, I guess I didn't."

"Instead, you just told her, let's keep talk of the wedding under wraps and things will be okay?"

Meagan groaned, closing her eyes. "I'm an idiot. She probably thinks I'm having second thoughts. She doesn't trust me but I didn't give her enough information to ease her fears. Do you think she believes I'm going to run out on her?" She paused, then said, "Never mind. She probably *does* because I didn't give her all the information."

"No shit, Sherlock. Get your ass home stat and tell her what's going on." I stood, grabbing Meagan's hand and pulling her to her feet. She was surprisingly heavier than she looked. "Ari's my best friend and she's devastated right now. Go undo the damage."

Wearing a contrite expression, Meagan nodded and headed for the door. "Thanks… I know I can be dense at times, but you'd think I wouldn't be this dumb."

"You aren't dumb. You just didn't think through how to handle it. Next time, examine everything you're planning." I shoved her out the door and immediately pulled out my phone to text Ari. MEAGAN'S COMING HOME TO TALK TO YOU. LISTEN TO HER. *I MEAN IT.*

After a few minutes, Ari texted back, ALL RIGHT. I WILL.

Satisfied that at least one problem was on the road to being solved, I headed back to the kitchen. I didn't feel like reading any more, and I wanted to keep my mind off the case. I decided to make chocolate chip cookies, just as my phone rang. It was Killian.

"Hey love, I know you're at work—"

"Actually, I'm not. Tad gave everyone the day off. It's a long story, so I won't go into it, but I have the afternoon free. I don't suppose you do?" I lowered my voice suggestively.

"I'm afraid I'm booked up," he said, and I could hear the wistfulness in his voice. "But I wanted to ask if I can come over tonight? Tally's going to visit a couple of her friends up in Bellingham, so I have the night free."

"Oh, please, come over. I need you." My entire body tingled at the thought. Killian was a skilled lover, and he wasn't so gentle that I felt like a porcelain doll.

"I'll see you at six-thirty, then? I'll pick up takeout on the way so you don't have to cook. What do you want?"

"Chinese," I said. "Don't forget the pot stickers."

"Will do." He paused, then added, "I miss you."

"Miss you too." I made kissing noises, and then hung up.

I made cookies, three batches, and then decided to tackle paying the bills and balancing my checkbook. After that, I watched a movie that I had been wanting to see that nobody else was interested in, and finally, when it was nearing six, I decided to change clothes and re-do my makeup.

I had just changed, into a black swing dress with white trim and silver buttons down the front of the sleeveless, sweetheart bodice, when the doorbell rang. I slipped into my sexy-librarian heels, which were a nice, chunky black satin matte with bows on the top, and descended the stairs to answer the door. I struck a pose and opened the door, expecting to find Killian there, early. But I was in for a shock.

There, on my doorstep, was Ellison.

"WHAT THE HELL DO YOU WANT?" I BLURTED OUT, WILLING him to vanish.

He snorted. "Nice greeting, January. Do you always meet your guests with such an eloquent salutation?"

I blinked. Unfortunately, he was really there. "My *guests* know they're always welcome in my home. You're not one of my guests. I repeat, what do you want?"

"Seriously, you aren't going to invite me in?" He looked so offended that I broke out into a peal of laughter.

"Ellison…if I could, I'd build a fence you'd never be able to scale." I stared at him, finally deciding that the only way to get rid of him would be to invite him in. "What the fuck. All right, you have five minutes before I kick your ass back out in the rain."

The evening was gloomy, the clouds socking in for a real downpour. In the Pacific Northwest, we had rainstorms where the rain came down sideways, pelting everything like sharp little bullets. The breeze was gusting and, as I stood back to make room for Ellison, I decided to get out the battery-operated candles and make certain I had wood for the fireplace in case of a windstorm. I hadn't checked the weather forecast in a while, but the day had a crackly feel to it, making my hair stand on end. *Thunderstorm weather...windstorm weather...*both were problematic.

Ellison hesitantly stepped through the door. He had only been to my house a few times, always making excuses to get out of visiting my parents and friends. Mostly, he had come here while we were in college at Western Washington University and he drove me home for the weekends. I had lived close enough to commute, but it was easier to just stay in the dorms during the week.

What Ellison lacked in grace and manners, he made up for in looks, but after spending ten minutes with him, the glamour faded when his personality emerged. He was a tall, lanky man, with wavy blond hair and sparkling blue eyes, but there was a coldness behind the sparkle, a sense of disdain for anyone and anything that he considered beneath his stature. While recent events had knocked him down a peg, the gratuitous snobbery remained.

"Get to the point. What do you want?"

He licked his lips, glancing around. "I haven't been here in a long time," he said.

"It wasn't for the lack of invitation. You refused to come to any event my parents put on. Even their funeral," I said, pointedly.

"Yeah, I'm...sorry about that. I know we were separated but I should have come with you." He was scrambling, I could see it.

"No, really, it's better you didn't. It cemented what a crummy person you really are. What do you want, Ellison?"

"You look nice," he said, and right then I knew he wanted something. He hadn't complimented me in a long, long time.

"Thank you. Now, what do you want?" There was a technique they taught in classes for self-assertiveness. It was called the "broken record technique." It involved acknowledging what the other person said, but then repeating your stance again, refusing to be sidetracked or gaslighted.

He let out a long sigh, turning on what I assumed were supposed to be puppy dog eyes. "I've been thinking a lot lately, about our marriage. About *you*." He paused, then asked, "Do you ever think about *us*?"

"Not so much. What do you want?"

Frowning, he cleared his throat. "Can you just let me talk?"

"Apparently, I learned how to talk over people from you, Ellison. You taught me that lesson well. Once again, *what do you want?*"

"Damn it, will you shut the fuck up and let me tell you that I miss you?" He was shouting.

I immediately pulled back and he froze.

He took a shaky breath and added, "I said I miss you, January. I was thinking...maybe we could give it another try? Maybe we could start a new magazine together?"

What the ever-loving hell? I stared at him, unable to process his suggestion. Was he really that dense? Was he really that *stupid*? As I stared at him, he rushed on.

"I thought that we could wipe the slate clean. Start new. We could start dating again—did I tell you how great you look? If things go all right, I could move in with you here—"

That brought me round and I found my tongue again.

"Put the brakes on. First, *you* left *me*. *I* didn't leave *you*. You're the one who cheated on me. *You're* the one who bilked me out of my half of the magazine. *You're* the one who did everything you could to prevent me from getting my fair share of our assets in the divorce. *You're* the one who found a judge you could bribe to overlook all the crap you pulled on me. I caught you with your head between another woman's legs. Dining out costs you, Ellison. So does treating me like dirt."

He stiffened, his eyes shifting. The cajoling look was gone, replaced by anger. I could recognize the signs—I had learned the hard way how to adjust my actions in seconds when he got into his moods. But this time, I wasn't going to smooth things over.

Hands on my hips, I glared him down. "You really think that I'd ever consider going back to you? That I'd ever even *think* of getting back together? The thought of your hands on me makes my skin crawl. I suggest you run home to Mama because as far as I'm concerned, she's the only woman willing to put up with your bullshit. Even your mistress learned that you're an asshole."

He leaned a little too close for comfort. "When did you become so cynical—"

"When you decided I was dead weight." I was over it —*Stick a fork in me* done. "I'm with a man who truly cares about me. Even better, *I* care about me. I spent eighteen years under your thumb. As Ricky Nelson said, *I've learned my lesson well.* So it's time for you to leave. I don't ever want to see you again. Got it?"

Frowning, Ellison cocked his head to the side. "I don't understand how you became so…so…"

"So *self-assertive*? I don't enjoy being a doormat, Ellison. I'll never again accept the kind of bullshit you threw at me. Good-bye." I started backing him up toward the door, and then when we were there, I opened it and pointed toward the sidewalk. "*Go home, Ellison.* Get out of my life."

He paused, then, his eyes narrowing, he turned toward the door. I thought he was going to leave. But instead, he reached out and slammed it shut. The look in his eyes shifted as he whirled around and shoved me up against the wall.

"Oh, you're not done with me yet. You think I hurt your poor little heart before? Think again. I'm going to teach you what it *really* means to hurt. Since you won't shut up, I'll shut that fat mouth for you!" And then, before I realized what he was doing, he took a swing at me.

I screamed and ducked, unable to believe what was actually happening.

CHAPTER TWELVE

*E*llison's fist met the wall as I swerved, just in time to avoid being hit. I didn't pause to respond. I ducked under his arm and away, as he struggled to shake the plaster off his knuckles. As I backed away, my anger boiled and I felt a knot of outrage growing in the center of my gut.

"How dare you come into my house and attack me?" My eyes blazing, I shook that knot of anger free and the next thing I knew, a glowing green globe shot out of my hand as I raised it to ward him off. The energy blob sailed across the foyer, landing hard against Ellison's chest. He let out a shout and stumbled back as the energy flared and exploded in his face.

I froze, not sure what had just happened.

At that moment, the door slammed open and Killian rushed in. He took one look at Ellison, one look at me, and then dragged Ellison up by his collar, snarling.

"Did you touch her?" Killian's voice was dangerously low.

Ellison began to babble and kick his feet as Killian held him up as easily as he might hold a kitten.

"*Did you try to hurt her?*" Killian asked again, his voice threatening. "I won't ask again."

"Killian, don't…" I started to say *Don't hurt him*, but then stopped, changing my words to "Don't *kill* him." I wasn't going to cover for Ellison ever again. I just didn't want Killian going to jail because of him.

"I didn't mean to—" Ellison started to say. That was as far as he got.

Killian dragged him out on the porch and down the stairs, ignoring Ellison's shouts as he flailed. Ellison's car was parked in front of the house—the convertible that I had filled with water when I walked out on him. Killian stopped at the end of the path, lifted Ellison in the air, and threw him onto the hood of the car. Ellison landed with a thud, groaning as he slid off and shakily tried to stand up.

"Get in your car and if I ever see you again in this town, I *will* kill you. And no jury in the land will convict me when I expose the crap you pulled on my mate." Killian pointed to the car door. "Don't say a word. Get in the car and *drive.*"

Ellison used the car to steady himself as he slid along the side, heading for the driver's door. "I— I… January," he said, turning to me, pleading.

"You'd better do as he says," I said. "Move it or lose it."

With a strangled curse, Ellison jumped into his car, and a moment later, pulled into the street and sped off.

Killian turned to me. "Are you all right?" he asked.

"I'll be okay," I said, as I started to shake. I was great in a crisis, but fell apart after it was over. "Ellison tried to punch me, but I managed to duck." I stared at the retreating tail lights. "I never expected him to try to hit me. He always yelled at me a lot, and insulted me, but… Maybe I didn't cave into his expectations. Maybe he really believed that I'd fall for his change of heart again, and when I didn't, he snapped." I told him about how quickly Ellison had gone from trying to persuade me to take him in to trying to cold-cock me.

"If he ever comes near you again, I guarantee, he'll vanish and nobody will ever know what happened." Killian wrapped his arm around me. "Are you sure you're okay?"

I nodded as we walked inside. "Yeah, but my wall isn't." I showed him where Ellison had swung at me and hit the wall instead. "I almost want to leave it in case I ever feel sorry for him again. Then I could just look at it and remember."

"Take a picture of it. You can use it in court if you like."

"That's a good idea—just to remind myself. Plus, I suppose I should call Millie and report the incident in case he decides to come back."

"Call her now, while I get dinner from my car and set the table." He paused. "I felt your fear—as I was pulling into my driveway, I felt your fear. We're *bonding*, January." He headed over to his driveway.

I called Millie and she made it to my house in record time. Who said the cops were never around when you needed one? I showed her the wall and told her what had happened.

"So, do you want to file a restraining order? Based on this, Judge Warrenson will have no trouble granting you one. I think you should do it, because then if he oversteps himself again, the punishment will go a lot harder. Also, cowards like Ellison usually think twice if they know the authorities are watching them." Millie took a couple pictures of the wall.

I nodded. "Yeah, I guess I should. What's the procedure?"

"Ask for a domestic violence order of protection—a DVOP—since the two of you were married. Go down to the courthouse tomorrow and put my name down on the forms as a contact, since I have pictures of the damage he did to your wall and took the report."

I paused. "Does it matter that Killian threatened him and threw him out?"

"Not if he was protecting you. Also, given you are Otherkin, I recommend that you ask the Court Magika what they can do. In a mixed marriage—where one person is human and the other not—sometimes there are other avenues that can be pursued." Millie glanced out the window. "Do you think he'll come back tonight?"

"I don't know. He'd be a fool to, after Killian got done warning him, but he seemed to have snapped, so I'm not sure what state of mind he's in."

"I'll call the police in…where's he live? Seattle?"

I shook my head. "He used to. He's living with his parents in Bellingham now." I looked up the Reilly address and gave it to her.

"All right, I'll call a couple of the cops I know in Bellingham and ask them to sit down with him and *explain* why he shouldn't set foot in Moonshadow Bay again." She stood. "By the way, please tell me that you aren't ever going back to him. I'm so tired of seeing women going back to their scumbag husbands and boyfriends who treat them like dirt."

I laughed then, relieved to have something to laugh about. "Oh Millie, if I never see him again, it will be too soon."

Satisfied with my answer, she excused herself and I shut the door behind her, locking it tightly.

Killian was waiting in the kitchen. He had brought Chinese food for dinner from Heavenly Garden Palace, one of the best Chinese restaurants in town. It was actually Chinese-American cuisine, but it was good. I loved their pot stickers and eggrolls.

"Millie's gone?" he asked, watching me closely.

I nodded, sitting down at the table and taking a long sip of the cold water he had poured. "Yeah. She recommends I file a restraining order and talk to the Court Magika to see what else can be done."

"What did you do to him? I could smell the ozone on his shirt." Killian sat down, dishing up a plateful of chicken fried rice and egg rolls and orange chicken.

"I don't know, to tell you the truth. I really need to set up that appointment with the Aseer to find out just what I'm capable of. I meant to, back around my birthday, but one thing and then another got in the way. But tonight when I was trying to defend myself, I got really angry and a ball of energy flew out of my fingers and hit him, knocking him back. It didn't feel like fire energy, but more…like I threw a rock at him. I'm not sure. I need to talk to Rowan. I wish she'd get back from her trip."

Killian nodded soberly. "Call the Aseer tomorrow, and also file for a restraining order and talk to the Court Magika. You can't let this slide. If Ellison's over the edge enough to try to hit you, then he's dangerous and it doesn't do to let danger go unanswered."

I promised. "Thank you for coming to help. Thank you for taking my side."

"I keep telling you, *you're my mate*. I don't think you realize what that means."

"Maybe I don't," I said slowly. I glanced around.

He mopped up some sauce on his plate with some of the rice. "Listen…I know we haven't officially talked about it, though I've already told you that I'm a one-woman man, but I'd like to clarify the state of our relationship. I don't want you seeing—*dating*—anybody else. Man, woman…either…I want exclusive rights to your bed. At least when it comes to sex and romance. Slumber parties with your girlfriends are none of my business."

I leaned back in my chair, smiling. "I thought we already agreed on that. At least tacitly."

"Ah," he said with a smile. "You never really answered me on that."

"Then let me put your mind to rest. I don't want to think of you kissing another woman—not like you kiss me. I want you all to myself, and I promise to be faithful to you as long as we're together." I leaned across the table and took his hand. "I didn't plan on a relationship so soon, but I've learned that sometimes fate has other ideas and it's usually wise to listen to them."

"Smart woman," he said, tenderly stroking my fingers. "Then it's settled. We're a couple, exclusive, and mated to one another."

"You keep using the word 'mated'…I know that's standard in shifter groups, but what exactly does it mean?"

He shrugged, a playful look on his face. "You're my love. My lover. My chosen one. I share my bed with you and you alone. And vice versa." Then, still holding my hand, he looked at me and, in a soft but serious voice, said, "I love you, January. I've fallen hard for you. I don't know where we're going, but I know that I want to walk on the path beside you."

I caught my breath. He had said the words—and he wasn't running away. "I love you, too," I said. "I've wanted to say that for a few weeks now, but I've been afraid that I'd scare you off."

"Oh, love. Never fear. If I run, it will be for other reasons. But I'm not planning on running away, and I don't plan on letting you get away, either, unless you're unhappy. I'll never try to force you to stay, but I hope you will." He brought my hand to his lips, kissing it.

And that was it—a quiet declaration that changed the nature of our relationship, and made me both break out in a cold sweat and sigh in relief.

KILLIAN STAYED THE NIGHT JUST IN CASE ELLISON CAME back, and we celebrated saying "I love you" in the best way possible—a hot round of sex, and then Ben & Jerry's while we watched late-night TV. I didn't care about having to get up early. It wasn't every day that the person you had fallen in love with said it back to you.

Before going to sleep, I slipped into the bathroom to take a quick shower and while I was there, I texted Ari. HE SAID HE LOVES ME. AND ELLISON TRIED TO CLOBBER ME.

That got an immediate response. DO YOU WANT ME TO CALL?

NO, BUT I'LL CALL YOU TOMORROW. MILLIE WANTS ME TO FILE A RESTRAINING ORDER AND THEN I NEED TO CONTACT

THE COURT MAGIKA AND ASK FOR AN AUDIENCE. HE'S NOT
GETTING AWAY WITH IT.

OKAY, BUT YOU'D BETTER CALL ME FIRST THING. BY THE
WAY, THANK YOU FOR TALKING TO MEAGAN. SHE TOLD ME
YOU SPOKE TO HER, AND SHE TOLD ME WHAT HAPPENED...
WE'RE OKAY. WE ARE KEEPING PLANS ON THE QUIET SIDE
UNTIL SHE GETS THE SEAL OF AUTONOMY, WHICH EFFEC-
TIVELY SEVERS HER BONDS WITH HER FAMILY. WE'LL GET
MARRIED. THEN, IF HER MOTHER TRIES ANYTHING, I CAN SUE
HER ASS OFF AND SHE'LL BE A LAUGHINGSTOCK IN HER PRIDE.

GOOD. I'M GLAD YOU WORKED THINGS OUT. I'LL CALL
YOU TOMORROW.

And with that, I finished taking off my makeup and
joined Killian in bed. He was already snoring away, and
for a long time, I just sat on my side of the bed, watching
him, wondering how we managed to find each other in
such a large, frightening world.

FIRST THING COME MORNING, I TEXTED TAD THAT I'D BE
late and I'd tell him why when I got there. Then I headed
down to City Central after feeding the cats. Killian was on
his way to work, and he suggested that I ask the cops to
drive by a couple times during the day to make sure the
house looked fine.

It was pouring rain, a real gully-washer, and the drops
pelted the ground, welling up on the pavement and shimmering under the streetlights. Daylight saving time guar-
anteed waking up in dark, at least at this time of year,
which I hated. I always felt like I was scrambling to find
that hour that had disappeared. I had signed every peti-

tion I could find asking the courts to abolish daylight saving time for good because it threw off my natural rhythms, but it looked like we were stuck with it for the foreseeable future.

I found the courthouse and filed for a DVOP like Millie had told me. I signed the forms, staring at the papers for a moment before turning them in. What I was doing would seal things between Ellison and me. But then again, him swinging at me had been the final straw. This was just the aftermath and he was the one who had brought it upon himself.

I stopped in to see Millie before I left City Central.

She was busy, but she smiled when she saw me and asked me back to her office. I declined to take up her time, but asked her if she could have an officer swing past my house a couple times during the day to check on things. They had Ellison's car make and model, and his license plate number, so they could see if it was anywhere along the block.

"Sure thing," she said. "I'm glad you took my advice. Too many women don't. They're afraid of making waves, or they don't want to hurt the guy's reputation, but that's just an invitation for him to try it again."

"I know," I said, shaking my head. "I can't believe it came to this, though. You know, I really thought that everything would be okay. I mean, yeah, he swindled me and he cheated on me, but I thought we could at least keep things on a semi-civil level."

She shrugged. "My guess is that when he had to sell the house, he decided to fix the blame on you. If you had taken him back, he would have made you miserable and punished you for everything he was angry over. Men like that are leeches. Well, I've also met some women like that, too, to be fair. Some people just can't shoulder the responsibility for taking care of themselves. They aren't stupid or incapable, they're just lazy and feel entitled. Ten to one, Ellison feels like you owe him the world."

"I already know he blames me for his misfortune. I don't know how he lives with himself."

"I'll bet he sleeps just fine at night. People like that do, until you rub their noses in their own piss, so to speak." She waved as I headed for the door. "I'll make sure to have a patrol car pass by your house a couple times today."

My next stop was the Court Magika building, which was located in a small brick building that had once been a house, on the corner of Elkwood and Hart streets. There was a parking strip in back of the building with enough room for about ten cars.

I parked, trying to dash between the raindrops around to the front where the entrance was. Though the sidewalk was partly covered by the eaves, by the time I made it to the door, my hair was wet through. I pushed through the front door of the renovated house, finding myself in a small reception room. It had probably been the living room at one time, but now it reeked of magic—in a good way—and all the furniture was utilitarian.

A woman was sitting behind the main desk, and she looked up from the magazine she was reading—*Spell-Casters Monthly*—and motioned for me to approach the desk.

"May I help you?"

I licked my lips, not sure how to proceed. "I live in Moonshadow Bay, and the chief of police suggested I talk to you about something that happened last night."

"Civil or legal?" she asked, turning to her computer. Her hair was light brown, down to her shoulders, and she looked about twenty, though chances were good she was older than that. She was stick-thin and had a nasal voice, reminding me of those cartoon secretaries with New Jersey accents and confetti for brains.

"Legal, I guess."

"All right, have a seat and please tell me what your concern is. If the police suggested you come here, then we'll need to start with Form 10-B, which we'll need to fill out and then I'll fax it over for a signature from the officer who recommended you seek our help." She suddenly turned no-nonsense.

I explained to her what happened, and that Millie, the chief of police, had suggested I come talk to the Court Magika. "I'm not sure why, given my ex is human, but I thought I would take her advice, just on the chance that you can help somehow."

"We take threats against our witchblood members of the community seriously, Ms. Jaxson, so you did right to approach us. Whether we can do anything or not, I don't know. But it's always a good idea to check in with us when threats like this are bandied around."

I told her everything that happened, including striking back at him. "By the way, do you know how I can contact the Aseer? I was never tested when I was younger—my mother expected I would after I reached eighteen, but I had moved away for college by then and never got around to it."

The Aseer was a member of the witchblood community who was the formal authority on what type of magic that individuals with witchblood were proficient in. Most witches were tested during childhood, but my mother wanted to give me a chance to develop my magical path fully. However, when I met Ellison, I stopped most of my practice, since it made him nervous.

If I had known he was like that at the beginning, I never would have married him—or I liked to think that I wouldn't have. But who knew? Young and stupid was often just young and stupid, no matter how we liked to think we were on top of things.

Melody—the receptionist—wrote a name and number down for me. "Here, this is the Aseer's email address. Just email her and ask for an appointment." She glanced over the form that we had filled out—her typing in the information as I gave it to her. "Is everything on this form true to your knowledge?"

I nodded. "Yes, I'll swear to it, if you need."

"No, just making certain we didn't miss anything," she said. She printed the pages and had me sign them, then filed her copy of the form away under a case number, to send to Millie for a signature.

"Is that everything?" I asked.

She nodded. "Yes, that's all. We'll be in touch as soon as the Council meets next month."

With that, I thanked her and left, wondering just what was going to come of this, if anything. Already more than an hour late for work, I stopped by an espresso stand for another latte, and headed out for Conjure Ink.

CHAPTER THIRTEEN

*B*y the time I got to work, Tad and the others were deep in conversation. They looked up as I entered the room. "Thank gods you've made it in," Wren said, jumping up. She, Caitlin, and Tad were sitting at the table. Hank was nowhere to be seen.

"What's going on?" I asked.

"Tabitha called. She's panicking. The baby vanished."

"What?" I shrugged out of my coat and sat down at the table.

"Zoey—or Zoey-replicant—has vanished. The window was open when Tabitha went in to check on her this morning and the baby was gone," Caitlin said. "She called us an hour ago. We would have called you but Tad said that you were taking care of important business. We sent Hank over to Tabitha's to see what he can find out."

"Crap, if it isn't one thing, it's another. I'm sorry I'm late, but my ex tried to take a swing at me last night and I needed to talk to the police and to the Court Magika this morning."

"Took a swing at you? Are you all right?" Tad asked.

I nodded. "Luckily, I managed to knock him back... and then Killian did the rest. But it was disconcerting, to say the least. But never mind that for now. Zoey is gone?"

Tad nodded. "She just seems to have vanished from the house. Tabitha thought she had locked all the windows and doors, but..."

I bit my lip. "The *mother*. The baby's mother—I'll bet you she came to get the baby." I looked over at the carousel. "I should have taken that over to Tabitha's yesterday instead of leaving it here."

"You don't know that it would have done anything," Caitlin said.

Wren shook her head. "Caitlin is right. But the problem now is, where is Zoey—the *real* Zoey? That's what we need to focus on."

I picked up the carousel, winding it and watching as the crystal unicorns danced around in circles. "I *know* the mother gave this to me for a reason. I wonder..." I paused, setting it down and closing my eyes while my hand was still touching the base. The toy was vibrating. It felt like it was almost singing against my fingers. "I think there's something..."

"What?" Caitlin asked, softly prompting me.

There was an idea forming in my head, but I couldn't quite pin it down.

"I don't know. I just believe that the mother of that baby didn't want to make the exchange. She missed her child, and...maybe she knows how much Tabitha misses her baby? Maybe she was trying to help us out?"

Sometimes, when an idea falls into place, there's a

click, an instinct that *yes*, things finally make sense. And that was what I was feeling now.

"I know that I'm on the right track," I continued. "The mother didn't want the exchange to happen. She's given us a key to finding Zoey. I think, given how much she loves her own child, that she recognized how upset Tabitha was."

"Why do you think she approached you and not Tabitha?" Tad asked.

I thought about it for a moment. "My great-grand-mother… She thought she lost a child to the Woodlings. Maybe it has something to do with that? I don't know."

"Then how do you think we should go about this?" Caitlin asked.

I thought for a moment. "I think I need to take the carousel into the woods near my home. The mother figured out how to contact me, so she might be watching. I need to make contact with the Woodling and maybe she'll lead me to Zoey."

"That could be dangerous," Tad said. "The Woodlings aren't known to be all that friendly to people. You aren't going alone."

"I could take Killian, but I have the feeling that the mother might show herself to women easier." I turned to Caitlin. "Would you go with me? The guys can wait on the lawn at the edge of the forest."

She nodded. "Yeah, I'll go. When do you want to head out?"

"This evening? Afternoon?" I glanced out the window. "We should talk to Tabitha first. I'm wondering, is there any information about when the Woodlings are more likely to show themselves?"

"The person who would probably know best about them is Rowan. But since she's out of town…let me think…" Tad walked over to his desk and pulled out an old-fashioned physical Rolodex. He began flipping through it, glancing at the names.

I turned to Caitlin. "So, how are you doing?"

She shrugged. "My parents officially disowned me today. Arlo's family is suing them for a severance dowry, even though Arlo asked them not to. He and I had a chance to talk and he told me that he respects my wishes —that he'd rather have a wife who is eager for marriage. It's a big mess, but there's not much I can do about it now."

I nodded, glancing over at Tad, who was still puzzling over the list of names. "Let me ask my aunt," I suggested. "She's been busy with spring planting, but she might know something about the Woodlings."

"Call her, please," he said. "I'm drawing a blank."

I called Teran. She answered on the second ring. "Hey sweetie, how are you?" She sounded a little out of breath.

"It's been a week. Say, do you know anything about the Woodlings? We've run into a problem…"

I could feel her mood shift, even over the phone. "You're mixed up with *Woodlings* now?"

"Yeah, and we could use some advice. Can you come down to the office, if you know anything about them that might help?"

She didn't hesitate. "I'll be right there."

I told the others she was on the way. "Call Hank and tell him to get back here. Do you think he should bring Tabitha?"

"I think that we need to keep her from running off

half-cocked, so yeah. I think that would be a good idea. She can wait in the outer room with Wren while we talk." Tad shoved the Rolodex back in his desk. "I have to know somebody with information about them, but I'm coming up with a total blank right now."

We milled around the office, taking care of minor things until my aunt arrived. Hank and Tabitha came trooping in shortly after that, and Wren escorted Tabitha out into the main reception area and closed the door firmly behind them.

We gathered around the table again. I brought Teran up to speed. My aunt was sixty-seven years old, but she didn't look a day over fifty, and she was more active than most twenty-year-olds. She had never married, instead choosing to date a string of men, and she had never shown any desire to have children. She was tall and sturdy, with long hair that she dyed depending on her mood—lately it had been black with electric blue streaks, but she told me that she was starting to think about green, for spring.

She gave me a peck on the cheek and sat down. Teran was in her overalls, and I could tell she had been working in the garden due to the dirt beneath her fingernails. She smelled like freshly turned soil and damp leaves.

"I'm sorry, I pulled you away from your garden, didn't I?" I asked. "Would you like some coffee?"

"Yes, and no. I just finished a latte on the way here." She paused, then added, "What have you gotten yourself into with the Woodlings? Hurry up, my lettuce won't plant itself."

Even though she sounded brusque, the truth was my aunt was one of the sweetest women alive. She had no time for idiots or foolishness, but she did like to have fun and sometimes she seemed younger than me.

I glanced at the others. "Well, we're working on a case. A changeling case."

"Uh oh." Teran paled. "I haven't heard of one of those in a while. You do realize they almost never turn out without heartbreak?"

I nodded. "So I gather." I explained what had happened, and then showed her the carousel. "I found this yesterday morning out in the yard. I'm wondering why the mother brought it to me."

"You're sure it was the mother?" Teran asked, gazing at me so intently that it made me nervous.

"No, I can't be positive. But it was out in the yard and Xi showed me the image of a Woodling—"

"Never assume, my dear. Never assume," Teran said, examining the carousel. She paused, turning it this way and that. "Did Esmara have anything to say about it?"

"She said human hands didn't make it."

"Maybe human hands didn't, but…" Teran paused. "You know there's talk in the family history that one of your great-grandmother's daughters was carried off by the Woodlings? The girl was never found."

I stared at her, startled. "Talk, or fact?"

"Talk, I think. But Colleen believed it to her dying day."

"Then you need to hear what I found in the attic." I told them about the book of shadows and what I had read about Lara. "So, why would the rumors still persist if they actually found Lara's body? Have you checked the ceme-tery to see if there's a headstone for her?" I was confused.

The rumors should have been put to rest with the discovery of Lara's body.

It was Teran's turn to frown. "I'm as confused as you are," she said. "I never heard the story that Lara was murdered. But then again, I've never seen Colleen's book of shadows. Are you *sure* that's what she said?"

"Yes, she didn't want to believe it. Also, Great-Grandma was jealous of Rowan Firesong. They knew each other and Rowan and Brian were pretty chummy, from what I gather. I'm not sure what, if anything, to ask when Rowan gets back from her trip."

Rowan Firesong had actually been my father's mother, unbeknownst to him. That made her my grand-mother, and she was from one of the strongest witch-blood families around. My father, Trevor, had grown up believing he was a Jaxson through and through, even though they had been his foster parents, not his biolog-ical kin. He was never told that, although my mother had known.

"You don't say," Teran mused. "Rowan was around during that time, though she was young—probably in her mid-twenties. I can imagine, if she was anything like she is today, that Colleen would find her intimidating. But Colleen was no slouch herself. She ruled the roost, from what I gather."

"I have a feeling a lot went on under the surface back then. A lot we may never know about." I still had no clue why my grandmother had needed to hide the fact that my father was her son. But she had, apparently out of concern for his safety.

"Would the Court Magika have any information on the family?" I asked.

"You want to stay away from them as much as possible—"

I had been debating whether to tell my aunt about Ellison, but it seemed like I'd have to, now. "Um, too late. I stopped there this morning to file a report."

It was Teran's turn to do a double-take. "Why? What on earth caused you to do that?"

I let out a long breath. "You're going to find out anyway, so I might as well tell you. Ellison showed up at the house last night and he took a swing at me." I told her what had happened both before and after Killian showed up. "Millie recommended I not only file for a restraining order, but that I consult the Court Magika, so I did."

Teran sat back in her chair, regarding me quietly. After a moment's silence, she said, "Ellison tried to hit you?"

I nodded. "Killian came in right then—right after I let some sort of energy ball. I've emailed the Aseer to set up that appointment. I've never thrown off energy like that before and I'd—"

"Oh, you'll want to do that. But back to Ellison. Was he drunk?"

I shook my head. "I don't think so," I said. "He was just being his usual self."

Teran looked so grave that I was beginning to get worried. But she said nothing about Ellison. Instead, she picked up the carousel again. "I have a feeling you're right. This holds the key to finding Zoey. I suggest we take this out into the Mystic Wood and wind it up."

I stared at the toy. "I thought it was a music box at first. It seems odd that it's not, given the unicorns circle the carousel." I held out my hand and took it from her. "I like holding it. I don't know why, but…"

Because it resonates with the woodland energy, and that resonates with Druantia's energy. Esmara chuckled. *You'll find you're much more in tune with the forests now that you have officially claimed service to Druantia.*

That makes sense. I paused, a thought crossing my mind. *Is that why the Woodling brought this to me? Did she sense my connection to Druantia? Are the Woodlings connected to her as well?*

Now you're using your brain, Esmara said. *Think it through. I'm here to guide you, not give you the answers.*

"The Woodling, she trusts me because she senses my connection to Druantia," I said. "It just hit me. That's why she brought this to me. Can we head out to the woods now? Teran, will you come with me?"

Teran nodded. "I can do that."

"Before we do that, we should talk to Tabitha," Tad said. He motioned to Hank, who popped out into the reception area and escorted Tabitha into the room.

She settled in at the desk, glancing nervously at Teran. "I don't think we've met."

"I'm Teran Karns, January's aunt," Teran said, extending her hand. She had a way of making people feel comfortable, and within minutes Tabitha was telling her all about Zoey and what had happened.

"All right, let's figure out what the timeline was," Tad said. "Tabitha, when you put Zoey down, was the window in her room locked?"

Tabitha shook her head. "I usually keep my windows and doors locked, but yesterday I aired out the nursery and I think I forgot to close the window."

"Then whoever stole the baby must have gotten in that way." He paused. "Did you call the police?"

She shook her head. "After what happened with them not believing me about the changeling at first, and then the doctor talking to the police chief—"

"Dr. Fairsight checked out the Zoey stand-in and verified that, beneath the glamour, the creature is a baby Woodling," I told Teran.

Teran nodded, turning back to Tabitha. "Go on."

"This morning when I found the baby gone, I was worried that the police might think I hurt her. But I wouldn't have hurt her. Not now that I understand what's going on. If I hurt their baby, they might hurt Zoey in return."

I didn't have the heart to tell her that wasn't the way the Woodlings usually worked. That if we didn't find Zoey and bring her home, chances were she'd end up a slave.

"We're going to see if we can find any trace of Zoey out in the Mystic Wood," I said. "My instinct tells me to go tonight, even though that's more dangerous. You are not coming along. I want you to go home and stay there, in case the mother returns with the baby."

Tabitha nodded. "What should I do while I'm there?"

"Just keep an eye on the nursery." I turned to Tad. "Do you mind if I take the lead on this? I'm going on instinct."

He shrugged. "That's fine. Go ahead."

I thought for a moment, then said, "Caitlin, Teran, and I will head into the Mystic Wood with the carousel. I wonder if Ari can get away." I put in a call to her and she said she'd come right over.

"Do you want Peggin to come with us? She's still in town and she's willing. And she's a damned good shot.

She carries a nine-millimeter Sig Sauer, which endeared her to no end with Meagan, who loves target practice."

"Bring her, if she's willing to follow orders. Make sure she's dressed for a hike in the woods. Meet us at my house." I disconnected, turning to the others. "Ari and her friend Peggin are coming along. My instincts tell me that women need to go into the wood…men are going to be rebuffed."

"Are Woodlings all women?" Tabitha asked.

Teran shook her head. "No, but the male members of their society stay quiet and in the background. They act as sentinels and guards while the women go out and do most of the work and gather their food and run their villages."

"What do they eat?" I couldn't imagine what kind of food they ate, given what little I had seen of them.

"They're omnivorous. Woodlings feed on just about anything. They mainly scavenge for their food and eat everything from leaves to mulch to rotting bodies of animals—and humans."

I shuddered. They seemed entirely alien to me, and I wondered just how far removed from our world they really were. But they were part of nature, part of the food chain and part of the life cycle. I tried to remember my mother talking about them, but I couldn't recall the subject ever coming up. She used to talk about "creatures" in the trees, but I had never expected "creatures" to be walking bushes. When I thought of beings out of the wood, I thought about Tolkien's Ents, but the Woodlings were like no Ent I had read about or seen in a movie.

We gathered up our things, and Hank volunteered to drive Tabitha home, and then meet us at my place.

"Will we need any equipment?" Tad asked.

I shook my head. "This is one time we aren't going to go in with cameras. We do that, and we probably won't see hide nor hair nor…branch…of a Woodling."

As we headed toward the parking lot, I kept thinking of the mother Woodling, and the look on her face when we chased her off from her baby. I knew she had brought me the carousel for some reason, and I hoped that I would have reason to thank her.

CHAPTER FOURTEEN

I was the first one to reach my house. I dropped my purse on the sofa, then changed shoes to a pair of hiking boots so I could tromp through the woods. I changed out my coat for a windbreaker and then scared up a pair of crocheted gloves that I could wash easily enough if they got too dirty.

Xi and Klaus were dozing on the sofa, and I scooped them up and carried them up to the guest room. I didn't want to take a chance on them getting out, so it made sense to give them a quiet time out where they couldn't slip between anybody's feet. One of their litter boxes was already in there, so I just added a bowl of water and a bowl of kitten kibble, and they were good to go. By the time I got back downstairs, Ari was there, sitting in the living room with Peggin.

I grinned at them. "Hey, you."

"I hope you don't mind us letting ourselves in," Peggin said, but I shook my head.

"Ari knows she can come and go as she pleases." I sat

down beside them as we waited for the others. "So, Ari says you carry?"

Peggin nodded. "I've taken a number of classes, and I target shoot regularly. I don't rely on my gun to solve problems, but it's there if I need it. Do you think I should leave it behind? I know sometimes, when I go into the woodlands surrounding Whisper Hollow, I have to be cautious where I take this." She patted her pocket.

"I think that it might be a good idea. Here, we can lock it up in my desk." I opened the bottom desk drawer and she carefully emptied the gun and put it in there. I locked the drawer and we locked the ammo up in another drawer.

"I normally carry it with me, but magical woodlands are an entirely different environment." She returned to her seat on the sofa. "My boyfriend...significant other? How old do we have to be in order to stop calling them our boyfriends?"

I laughed. "I don't know. I'm forty-one, and I call Killian my boyfriend."

Peggin grinned. "I'm forty-three. My SO is called Dr. Divine—"

"A doctor?" Somehow I couldn't picture Peggin with a white-coated medical professional.

Peggin snorted. "Oh, no. D-D isn't *that* kind of a doctor. Um...someday you'll have to meet him. He's an artist."

At that point, our conversation was interrupted by the doorbell. It was Tad and Caitlin. Hank would arrive as soon as he dropped off Tabitha, and my aunt was also on the way.

I wandered into the kitchen where I retrieved the

cookies I had baked and spread them out on a plate, carrying them into the living room.

Peggin perked up. "Love those!"

Ari laughed. "Cookies. Of course. Got any wine to go with them?"

"We're not getting drunk. We're not even getting mildly *tipsy*. At least until we're out of the Mystic Wood." I set the cookies down and answered the door again. Teran had arrived and, behind her on the walk, Hank was striding through the rain. I let them in, relieved that we were all here and ready.

"How's Tabitha doing?" I asked Hank as he passed me by to enter the living room.

He shrugged. "I think she'll be okay, but she's definitely having some issues processing everything. Losing this child, even though it was a changeling, seems to be triggering her just as badly as losing Zoey did. She seems to feel even guiltier."

"Crap. I wish she wouldn't. I can guarantee you that if one of the Woodlings wants a child, they're going to find a way to nab it." I scratched my head. "So, otherwise, though? Do you think she's okay?"

"Otherwise, well…she's doing as well as we can expect her to be, I guess." He glanced around. "Nice place."

"Thanks, I grew up here."

"Local yokel, then?" He grinned as he said it and any sting slipped away.

I nodded. "About as local as you can get. My great-grandfather helped found this town, you know. I thought I told you that."

"You probably did, but I don't always file away everything I hear. My brain already feels fuller than I can handle at times." Hank winked at me.

I glanced around the room. "It looks like we're all here, so why don't we head out? There are lawn chairs on the back porch, and Hank and Tad, you might want to bring them along so you can sit while you wait for us." I glanced around, wishing I knew how to use a weapon. I was rethinking asking Peggin to leave her gun in my house. "Do you think we'll need weapons? I'm not comfortable with Peggin bringing a gun, but…"

"Face it, January, if things gets physical, we're screwed." Ari laughed, then sobered quickly. "Seriously, I wouldn't even know how to *begin* to fight against something like a Woodling. I doubt if you can shoot them, because we don't even know if they have any internal organs. Has anyone ever seen one bleed?"

I shrugged. I had no idea what the inner anatomy of the Woodlings looked like. Given how treelike they were, I wondered if their veins contained sap rather than blood. "I'm not even sure if it's safe to carry an ax or a hatchet into the wood."

"At the least, take a whistle and your cell phones in case you run into trouble. If you can't use your phone for any reason, blow loud on the whistle so we can hear." Tad still didn't look happy about being left behind.

"That we can do. I actually have a whistle for when I walk out at night alone. I haven't had to use it since I moved back from Seattle, but I always wore it when I took a walk at night in the city streets." I dashed upstairs to my jewelry box, where I found the whistle. I was just about to return downstairs when Killian texted me, asking what I was up to.

I'M HEADED INTO THE MYSTIC WOOD WITH ARI, TERAN, CAITLIN, AND PEGGIN. WE'RE HEADING OUT LOOKING FOR ZOEY. THE MOTHER WOODLING KIDNAPPED HER OWN BABY BACK FROM TABITHA, AND SHE SEEMS TO HAVE LEFT ME A CLUE.

DON'T YOU DARE GO UNTIL I GET THERE, Killian texted back.

WE'RE NOT TAKING THE MEN WITH US, WE HAVE THE FEELING IT WOULD BE AN UNWISE MOVE. BESIDES, YOU HAVE TO WORK.

That didn't go over well at all. Killian texted me that he was coming right home and again warned me not to go into the wood without him. Once again I told him that we were headed out *now*, but if he wanted to come wait with Tad and Hank, he was welcome.

Hoping that he wouldn't be too angry, I headed back downstairs so that we could get the show on the road.

THE RAIN HAD LESSENED, BUT TAD AND HANK SET UP umbrellas over their lawn chairs. I glanced at the other women, who seemed to be waiting for my lead. I took a deep breath and plunged into the wood. The others followed. We were all apprehensive, and it took some effort for us to spread out rather than cluster together.

A few birds were chirping, singing their rain songs, which echoed with the melancholy sound throughout the Mystic Wood. Raindrops dripped from the branches, landing on the forest floor with soft plops. The smell of cedar and fir permeated the air, along with damp soil pungent with the aroma of spring.

Each season had a scent. Spring always seemed a little fetid as new growth pushed through the soil, waking up from the long winter's nap. Summer smelled dusky and dusty, in a lazy sort of way. Everything smelled warm, as the flowers filled the air with their heady intoxicating scent. In the autumn, the smell of smoke and cinnamon filled the air, and the boreal winds carried in the presage of winter. And then in winter, everything smelled crisp and clear, harsh and bracing and sharp.

I paused, looking around, trying to listen for the heartbeat of the forest. Closing my eyes, I whispered a small prayer to Druantia. *Please help me understand the forest. Guide me in the way I should go.*

The next moment, I felt the urge to pull out the carousel. I raised it up and slowly wound the key so that the unicorns were dancing in a circle. As I held it out, in the palm of my hand, I slowly began to make out a faint sound like flutes playing on the wind. Listening closely, I reassured myself that yes, I was actually hearing what I thought I was. I tried to discern the direction from which the song was coming.

"Do you hear that?" I whispered to Teran, who was standing right behind me.

My aunt nodded, scanning the wood in front of us. "I can hear it. It started when you wound the carousel."

"Can you tell which direction the music is coming from?"

She closed her eyes, trying to pinpoint the origin of the sound, then shook her head. We turned to the others, who were also looking around.

"It's coming from the northwest," Peggin said. "Is there a path in that direction?"

I gazed at the undergrowth surrounding us, bordering both sides of the path. Then I paused, spying what looked like an old trail leading to the northwest. It was covered up by ferns and skunk cabbage, but when I pushed them aside, I could see that it had once been an actual path. I took a deep breath and stepped off the main trail.

We pushed our way through the undergrowth, side-stepping the rocks and twigs that littered the ground until we came to a set of twin firs, one on either side of the path. They towered overhead, straight as arrows, massive sentinels in the center of the forest. I knelt by the base to examine their roots, which were knotty and knobby. There was something that drew me to them, and I could practically hear Druantia egging me on.

Then I saw it. There, nestled in between two roots, was a small metal octagon. It was flat, with equidistant ridges spreading out from the center. I stared at it for a moment. It reminded me of something. Then the sound grew louder and, startled, I glanced at the carousel in my hand.

Bingo!

Everything clicked. I slowly fit the carousel down on the metal piece, aligning the furrows on the underside with the ridges on the metal base, and it fit perfectly. The carousel began to spin faster, and I jumped back. Between the trees I could see a web of light. It looked like a spider's web, only it was made up of shimmering strands.

"What's that?" Ari whispered.

I shook my head. "I think…it's a door."

"To where?" Peggin said.

"To where the Woodlings live? Maybe?" My stomach

knotted as I gazed at the shimmering lights. I called out for Esmara, hoping she would be there. *Should we go through?*

I cannot tell you what lies beyond because I don't know. But you were led here, so...try. There are some risks in life we need to take.

I glanced back at Teran. "Esmara thinks we should try."

"I think...you were led to this path. Anybody who's uncomfortable going should stay here." My aunt put her hand on my shoulder. "I'll go with you, sweetie. I have your back."

I caught my breath and nodded. "All right. Peggin, Ari, Caitlin? Don't feel you have to come with us. I'd rather you stay if you don't feel comfortable. I don't want to be responsible for leading anybody into something they might not come back from...at least in one piece."

Part of me couldn't believe I was actually saying this. Part of me sort of believed it was all some weird dream and I'd wake up and we'd be stoned off our asses, watching *Lord of the Rings* or something equally as fantastic. But the reality was we were here, in the middle of the forest, trying to decide whether to step through what appeared to be a portal between dimensions.

"I'll go," Peggin said.

Ari and Caitlin nodded. "We're game. Let's do it."

Swallowing my fear, I turned back to the web of light. "All right."

Holding my aunt's hand, I closed my eyes and stepped between the trees, half-expecting to be electrocuted.

THE NEXT MOMENT, I OPENED MY EYES AND QUICKLY scanned around me. Aunt Teran was standing beside me, and behind us, the two fir trees still stood tall, with the light between them, but we couldn't see the others. The wood looked exactly the same, except Peggin, Ari, and Caitlin were nowhere to be seen. I cocked my head, staring at the portal, and the next moment, Peggin jumped through, then Ari and Caitlin followed.

"Well, wherever we are, it's very like the Mystic Wood we just left behind," I said, startled as my words rang out, then seemed to vanish. It was as though I had shouted into a wind tunnel and the breeze had caught my words up and raced off with them.

The forest looked to be the same, only there was a difference to the way it felt. And there was something else, too. Everywhere I looked, I seemed to see shimmers in the air. I tried to focus on one, but it darted away the moment I thought I had it in sight. The dancing lights flew erratically, zipping like fireflies, but I knew they weren't like any insect I had ever seen.

"What next?" Ari asked after a moment. Her words, like mine, seemed to float on the breeze for a second and then were snatched away. It was almost as though they were out of sync with the movement of her lips.

"Strange," I murmured. I closed my eyes again and reached out to Druantia. It felt like this would be a place I could commune with her much easier.

What should we do? I asked.

Move forward. Follow the path. It will lead you to where you need to go, came the reply. It wasn't Esmara speaking, nor my own subconscious, so I decided to accept that it was Druantia and leave it at that.

I began to walk forward on the path, motioning for the others to follow me. We stayed silent, and I could tell the others felt as uneasy as I did about talking aloud here. Who knew what—or who—was eavesdropping on our conversation?

The path led through the woods, much more clearly delineated than the side path had been on the other side of the portal. Here, it was neatly trimmed back and I kept having visions of wandering through the woods to a gingerbread house. Only this time, *I* was the witch. So would Hansel and Gretel be the ones living inside in this twisted faerie tale?

We had been walking for about ten minutes when we came to a fork in the road, the two tines leading left and right. I stood there for a moment, closing my eyes, and I "saw" the right side of the road light up. I turned right without a word, hoping I was making the correct decision.

Another ten minutes and I became aware of the fact that we were being followed. Without a word, I held my hand up, coming to a stop, and the others stopped behind me. I turned around, leaning around them to scan the path behind us, but I could see no one there. But I knew— deep in my heart—that we weren't alone. After a moment, when nothing showed itself, I turned back to the path and continued on.

WE HAD BEEN WALKING FOR ABOUT HALF AN HOUR WHEN I spied a pool up ahead. Actually, it was a pond, surrounded by cattails, with waterlilies floating on the surface. The water didn't seem to be stagnant, like most ponds, and I wondered if it was being fed by an underground stream. Remembering that some of the Fair Folk from legend who lived near ponds and lakes weren't actually inclined to be fair, I stopped before we reached the edge of the water.

"Don't go near the water till we know it's safe," I said, the words dissipating as soon as they were out of my mouth.

"I'm beginning to wonder if we'll be able to find our way back," Ari said.

"We just turn around and go the way we came. The path is clearly marked." I shook my head. "There's a reason we're being led in this direction—" I paused as the sound of a child crying filled the air. "Hear that?"

"Yeah, but you remember the legends of the kelpies? They lured people in to drown through illusion," Teran said. Apparently her mind had been headed in the same direction mine had.

"I know, but…no…we need to find the source of the crying, although I do agree we should avoid the pond. The sound is coming from up ahead, to the left—away from the water." A sudden urge to run hit me, and I began to jog down the path, swerving away from the water. Teran followed me, then the others joined in.

I rounded a curve in the path and skidded to a stop. There, ahead in a clearing, sitting on a large boulder, was the mother Woodling I had seen before. She was holding her baby in one arm—which now looked like a Woodling —and beside her, bundled in what looked like a makeshift car seat, was Zoey, or at least I assumed it was her. The mother Woodling looked up to see us standing there, and she slowly motioned for us to come toward her.

CHAPTER FIFTEEN

*T*eran let out a little gasp. "I never thought I'd see one of the Woodlings," she whispered. "They're so…beautiful."

And *beautiful* was the word for it, though not beauty like we normally thought of. The mother and baby looked like willow wands twisted together, as though they were walking bundles of twigs. I kept thinking of a wicker chair, where all the canes were neatly laced together.

The mother Woodling had breasts—her baby was suckling on one—and she had almond-shaped eyes that glowed with a leaf-green light. Her lips were bowed, but they looked almost as though they were made of flower petals, and her hair trailed down her back, long streamers of ivy and leaves. I had seen some art created by sculptors that reminded me of this—like a tree come to life, humanoid and yet alien, and so completely natural that it seemed like we should see them in every park and forest.

Zoey, on the other hand, was hiccupping. She looked fully human—rosy cheeks and all. She was strapped into the makeshift seat with what looked like a belt woven of leaves.

I glanced at Teran. "Should I?" My voice shattered the silence of the woodland.

She nodded. "Go. You're the one that the Woodling gave the carousel to."

I moved forward slowly, hands out to show I carried no weapons. "Can you understand me?" I asked.

The mother looked up, and in what sounded like perfect English, said, "I can, January Jaxson. So you found the key."

I nodded, assuming she was talking about the carousel. "I found the key, yes. Is that the real Zoey?" I pointed toward the baby.

"Yes. This is the child my kind stole from the woman." Her face, so stoic and wooden, suddenly took on contours and I could have sworn she looked about ready to cry. "I stole her back from them. You need to take her away. I have to leave the forest with my child. Tell the woman I thank her—no, value the fact that she looked after my daughter."

I glanced around, looking for any signs that we were being observed. The feeling that we were being watched had stayed with me, and it made me uneasy. "Are you in trouble?"

The mother seemed to debate for a moment whether she wanted to talk with me, but then she nodded. "I'm in a great deal of danger now, from the Overkings."

That was a new one. I frowned. "Overkings?"

"Those who control all spirits in the woodlands. The children of the gods."

Teran stepped forward to stand beside me. "Are you talking about the Tuatha de Dannan?"

Again, the Woodling nodded. "They send us to steal the children, and we're forced to give up our own as changelings. This child," she said, pointing to Zoey, "was supposed to be delivered to them next week, after we had settled her in and made certain she was well enough that she wouldn't grow sickly on them. But I…" She glanced down at her own child, holding it protectively. "*I couldn't…*"

"You couldn't let them take your baby, either. You know how Tabitha feels." I felt a sudden rush of pity in my heart, and I turned to Teran. "We have to help her. We can't just take Zoey and leave…" I turned back to the Woodling. "What's your name?"

"Elsbet. My baby's name is Zera."

"We can't just leave them to fend for themselves." I glanced at Elsbet. "What happens to you if your people catch you?"

She gave me a calm, collected look. "They will kill me and take my child, and find another to exchange with. It will not be Zoey, however. Once a changeling leaves the Mystic Wood, they can never be collected again by our people. If they escape—however they escape—Druantia gives them a mark of protection."

I glanced around, wary. "How long do we have before they find you?"

"I cannot say. As soon as they realize the human child is missing, they'll begin the search. They make rounds three times each day to feed and hold the children. The third round will come near dusk."

"They only feed the babies three times a day?" Peggin asked, looking horrified.

"The children are taught to stop screaming…" Elsbet said, a catch in her voice. "The *tʊəhə deɪ ˈdanən* do not condone misbehavior."

I couldn't quite catch what she said, but Esmara whispered, *The Tuatha de Dannan, in an old tongue.*

"If we can help you escape, will you come with us? I know you can leave the Mystic Wood, given you have been in my backyard, and in Tabitha's house." I wanted to do something to help her. Elsbet had put her life on the line to return Zoey to Tabitha.

"If I may bring my Zera."

"Of course," I said. "Zoey and Zera sound very similar."

"That's because they targeted Zoey early on—the human girl has a great deal of latent power, even though she is not witchblood. So when my baby was born, they made me name her 'Zera,' so the sounds would be similar enough and she would respond to 'Zoey.' "

"Come with us," I said as Ari slipped forward to gather Zoey out of the seat. "We'll leave now. I'm not sure where we can hide you until we can move you, but…"

"She can come back to Whisper Hollow with me," Peggin said. "I doubt if there's much communication there—and if we have Woodlings over there, I've never seen them." She turned to Elsbet. "Do you know if there are any of your kind over on the Olympic Peninsula? Near Whisper Hollow?"

Elsbet frowned. "I don't recognize the name—"

"Near Lake Crescent?" Peggin asked.

That brought a response. Elsbet shivered. "No, the Woodlings leave those forests alone. The forests there are older than the Mystic Wood, and filled with dangers. If there are any Woodlings there, they're loners."

"Then if you come with me, you can settle in there. In fact, my boyfriend has a patch of woods right near his house. You could live there. I can't promise your safety—Whisper Hollow is a dangerous town—but you'll be in more danger here, I think."

I had the feeling we needed to get a move on. "Whatever you decide, make it fast. I have a sense that danger's on the way."

Elsbet nodded, standing. "I will go with you."

As we turned to leave the clearing and retrace our steps, there was a sudden sound from the other side of the lea as four very large, very imposing Woodlings stepped out of the tree line. They looked male, from what I could tell, and they also looked determined. They reeked of danger.

"Move!" I said, hustling Elsbet and her baby in front of us. "Hurry up. Head for the portal."

Ari, carrying Zoey, followed her. Peggin was next, then Teran, Caitlin, and I brought up the rear. Caitlin let out a snarl.

"Don't shift," I warned her. "Bobcats are nothing to tangle with, but I have a feeling these guards could easily take you on and win."

"Good thinking," Caitlin said. "Still, you go ahead and I'll take up the rear. I know martial arts and I'm good in a fight."

We hustled down the path, past the pond. As we passed by the water, the guards behind us blew a horn and there was a sloshing sound as something—a huge bloblike creature—oozed out of the water. Once on land, hundreds of spidery feet emerged from the pendulous beanbag of a creature, and it headed our way.

"A *dekta*," Elsbet shouted. "Don't let it touch you—its body is covered with a toxic slime."

Oh lovely, I thought. *A dekta, of course! Why not?* I found myself longing for last month, when all I had to face was a shadow man and a bunch of hostile ghosts.

We shifted into high gear and were jogging along as fast we could. The dekta, however, could ooze along on its numerous tiny feet like a millipede—and it moved at a good clip.

Too frightened to think about how terrified I actually was, I forced my feet to carry me as fast as I could. Ari, still carrying Zoey, had a good lead, and Elsbet was far faster than I would have imagined her to be. But Peggin, Teran, and I weren't all that quick on our feet, and Caitlin was sticking near the back to help us.

I glanced over my shoulder. The guards were catching up. They could move faster than we could and it wouldn't be long before they had hold of us. I wondered what they would do to us. We knew they would kill Elsbet, but what about witchblood?

I tried to think of any spells I might have that I could cast while on the run. The ball of energy the other night had been pure reflex against Ellison's attack.

"The whistle! What about your whistle?" Teran said as she gasped her way along beside me. I was worried about her. Sixty-seven wasn't as old as it used to be, but Teran had never been a jogger, and while she exercised, that didn't mean running through the woods with some crazed wood spirits after us was a piece of cake.

"Can they hear it on the other side of the—" I stopped,

skidding to a halt. Right beside us, emerging from the bushes, was a massive wolf. He was beautiful, with brilliant green eyes. "*Killian!*"

Killian leaped forward, landing between Caitlin and the guards, who were almost within arm's reach. He let out a low growl, and the next moment, he was joined by another wolf—smaller but just as menacing. This wolf was also gray, looking a lot like him, and had topaz eyes. Together, they blocked the path, their snarls enough to make my skin crawl.

"Run," Caitlin said, pushing me forward. "The portal's right there!"

I turned back to see that we had, indeed, made it back to the portal. As I watched, Ari and Zoey vanished through it, followed by Elsbet and her baby, and then Peggin darted through. I pushed Teran toward it.

"Go, I'll be right there."

"I'm not leaving you here—" she started to say, but I didn't give her the chance. I pushed her through, then followed.

The next moment, we stumbled through the shimmering light. Up ahead on the path, headed toward the place where we had forked off the main trail, were the others. I grabbed Teran's hand and shoved her forward as Caitlin came bounding through the portal. The next moment, both wolves came leaping through, and I grabbed the carousel off of the metal bracket.

As the shimmer flared—meaning the guards were following us through—it suddenly died and the web of light vanished.

We were alone in the forest.

I STARED AT THE TREES, WAITING, BUT NOTHING HAPPENED.
Apparently they didn't have a key to activate it from the
other side. They had probably expected to nab us without
much of a fight. Breathing hard, I leaned over, trying to
catch my breath. The larger wolf rubbed up against me,
whimpering softly. I patted his head and kissed it.

"Thank you," I whispered. "Thank you. Let's get out of
here before they find a way to open the gate."

With both wolves keeping guard behind us, we headed
toward the entrance to my yard. Once there, I turned
back to the trail, waiting for a moment. I spread out my
arms, instinct taking over, and envisioned a large field of
light shimmering along the tree line that bordered my
property.

> *Creatures of the woodland realm,*
> *If you unfriendly be,*
> *Stay on your side, behind this veil,*
> *And leave my yard to me.*

It wasn't poetry, but it should do the trick, I thought,
as I wove the veil of protection across the border to the
Mystic Wood. An influx of energy rippled across the back
of the lot, a shimmering veil of pale blue light. There was
a sudden hush—all sound fell away, and the world was
muffled like in a deep snow as the spell took hold. I could
feel Druantia there, shoring up my magic, and then it
settled into the ground, and things were back to normal.

I turned around and saw Ari, who was still holding
Zoey, standing next to Elsbet and her baby. The Woodling

took on a different look—here, she looked more like when I had first seen her. An elliptical head, sideways, atop a short, sinewy body.

"You look different," I said.

"Outside our natural realm, all Woodlings take on a different form." She was shivering. "I feel vulnerable here."

"Let's get you inside. We need to call Tabitha and have her come over." I began to herd people back inside the house, wondering what to do next. We had found Zoey, but I had the feeling that things weren't wrapped up just yet.

Killian and the other wolf bounded up the stairs and there, on the floor of the porch, I saw two piles of clothing. I gathered them up and motioned for the wolves to follow me inside. Once there, I led them upstairs and put one pile of clothing in my bedroom—the ones I recognized as Killian's. The other, I carried to the downstairs bathroom with the other wolf following. The clothes were made for a woman, that much I could tell.

My mind whirling with the events of the evening, when I showed the smaller wolf into the powder room and set her clothes on the counter, she let out a whimper. I looked down at her, puzzling. She felt familiar, but I wasn't sure whether I knew her or not.

"You get dressed and join us in the living room." I shut the door behind me.

Back in the living room, Hank was talking to Tabitha on the phone, while Elsbet and her baby were sitting quietly to one side, looking around the room. Tad and Caitlin were trying to warm up by the fireplace, which Ari had set alight. Ari had given Zoey to Teran, who was rocking her gently. The smell of baby poop filled the air, and both babies were fussing.

"I don't have any diapers on hand," I said, grimacing.

"Tabitha's bringing some. I told her we have Zoey. By the way, are we sure this is actually Zoey and not another changeling?" Hank asked.

"It's the human's child," Elsbet said from her corner.

I turned to her. "We can't let you be seen walking around town. If you can glamour up that way, can you somehow imitate a human?"

Elsbet cocked her head again, looking weary and bewildered. I could read the expressions, even on a face as alien to what I was used to. "I can, I suppose, though it's a difficult form to hold for long."

Peggin glanced at her watch. "I'm going to cut my trip short and head back to Whisper Hollow tonight." She sounded a little nervous and it suddenly occurred to me that she was taking quite a risk, ferrying them over to the peninsula. Hank glanced at her, then at the Woodlings. He must have sensed her concern as well.

"I can go with you," he said. "In fact, I'll drive them over, following you. That way I can get back home without a problem, and I'm pretty sure my car is bigger than yours, if you're driving that tiny little hybrid car I saw in the driveway."

The look of relief on Peggin's face was obvious. She let out a long breath. "Thank you. Yes, I do have a small car, and…" She closed her mouth.

"And we are not a known quantity," Elsbet said. "I can feel your reservations, and I understand them. I value you offering to help me in any way—especially when I aided in the theft of the child. Most of my kind would feel no remorse, but I have never been comfortable with exchanging children. But the *tʊəhə deɪ 'danən* beat and kill us if we do not obey. They're a cruel people, even those of the light. The *gods* are not as cruel as the Overkings, nor as arrogant."

I stared at her for a moment, thinking if the Fae were this deadly and without conscience, that I really didn't want to meet any of them. *Ever.*

Peggin blushed. "I really don't want to make you feel—"

"Do not worry about my feelings. Woodlings view the world from a different perspective." Elsbet turned to Hank. "Your presence would be welcome."

I started to say "Thank—" but Elsbet interrupted.

"I give you a word of advice, all of you. Do not thank any of the Fair Folk—the Overkings—or their servants. And the Woodlings are among their servants. Should you thank any of us, it indicates you owe us a favor, and we *will* collect on it, or cause havoc should the favor go unfulfilled. It is our nature. Again, I tell you this as a courtesy. And a warning for the future." She went back to her baby just as the doorbell rang.

Hank was nearest, so he answered. As he talked in hushed tones to whoever was there, Killian entered the room, looking freshly showered, and dressed. Behind him, from the hall bath, Tally followed. I blinked. *Of course* —his sister. That's why the wolf had reminded me of Killian.

"Tally! I didn't know that…" I let my words drift off, realizing that I had been jealous.

As the two wolf shifters crowded into the now-full

living room, Hank led Tabitha in. She took one look at Teran, who was holding Zoey, and let out a shout.

"Zoey! My baby!" As Tabitha made a beeline for her child, Zoey let out a gurgling sound and the little girl opened her arms wide and began to jabber. The reunion made me tear up, even though I wasn't all that child-oriented. I'd make a great auntie, but I couldn't really see myself as a mother. And since I was already forty-one, I had my doubts if I'd ever decide to enter the gene pool.

Tabitha turned and froze as she spotted Elsbet and her baby. She looked hesitant, but then walked over to the pair, handing Zoey back to Teran before she did so. Elsbet slowly stood, her back to the wall, shielding her child.

"Hank explained to me that I can't thank you for watching over my baby. He also explained to me that you had no choice in what happened. So…I won't thank you for taking care of Zoey, but I want you to know…I realize you did what you could, and I understand you put your life on the line by bringing her back to me." Tabitha paused. I could tell she was shivering.

Elsbet gave her a long look, then nodded. "I understand what you are saying. I wish…that none of this had been necessary."

Tabitha sniffed. "I think both our children need changing. I brought extra diapers. Would you like to clean her up?"

Elsbet broke into what looked like a smile. "That would be a good thing to do."

"I'll come with you both," Hank said. He seemed awfully protective around Tabitha, and I wondered if he had developed feelings for her. He seemed more involved in the case than usual. He and Teran went with Tabitha and Elsbet. Teran led them into the kitchen, where they would have room to clean both children.

I turned back to the others. "I'm glad Hank is going to be the one driving them." I looked at Peggin. "Are you sure they'll be welcome over in Whisper Hollow?"

"No," Peggin said. "But they'll be killed if they stay here. At least the mother will be. Since the Woodlings don't have an enclave over on the peninsula, they'll be able to create a home in the thicket near D-D's house—my boyfriend's house. We can watch over them as much as possible." She paused. "I think that while Moonshadow Bay and Whisper Hollow seem very much alike in a number of ways, there are definite differences." She paused. "Vampires, for one. Ari tells me you actually have them here?"

I nodded. "Yes, they live mostly out in the open here. Don't you have them over there?"

"We have what are called the UnLiving. But they aren't vampires. If we do have any, they stay hidden. But we have other creatures that I doubt I'd find over here. A lot of individualized...I suppose you could call them *monsters*? Entities?"

I glanced at Tad. "I really want to take a trip over to Whisper Hollow some time."

"My best friend used to work for a paranormal e-zine in Seattle," Peggin said. "She was a barista by day, and at night she used to go out investigating ghosts and haunted houses. It kept her powers from imploding. Spirit shamans have to use their abilities or they run into trouble."

"Same with witchblood," I said. "I had constant headaches with my ex, since he really didn't like me using my magic. It wasn't as bad as what it sounds like spirit shamans go through, though. I'd really like to talk to your friend at some point."

"We'll make a date," Peggin said.

Just then, Tabitha and Elsbet returned, both with happy, sleepy babies. Elsbet returned to her stance in the corner, while Tabitha settled on the sofa with Zoey.

I turned to Elsbet. "You said that Tabitha won't have to worry that they'll return for Zoey?"

Elsbet nodded. "That's correct. Zoey is marked. She's escaped the realm of Faerie, and so she's given automatic immunity. The Fair Folk won't ever bother her—or you, Tabitha—again. You can go about your life without that worry."

Tabitha's face crinkled into a smile. "Thank…heavens. I'm thinking I may move, though. This has all been such a shock, and I'm thinking a nice condo in a tall building in the city might be more to my liking."

Teran let out a sigh. "Don't let this drive you away. Moonshadow Bay isn't for everyone, but you were happy here until this happened, right?"

Tabitha nodded. "Yes, but this is going to be hard to leave behind. Thank you all—January, Hank, Tad, Caitlin…but I'm going to take my daughter and spend the night at a hotel. I don't think I can face going home just now. Too many raw memories from the past few weeks."

Peggin stood. "We should go, too. They'll be looking for Elsbet, and I have no idea if they're capable of trying to run us off the road. Hank, are you prepared to drive tonight? We'll have to take a ferry over to Kingston from Edmonds and then drive up the interior of the peninsula and along the highway until we come to Whisper Hollow.

It's going to take awhile so we need to leave now if we hope to catch the last ferry out. Luckily, I just have to pack up a few things at Ari's and I'll be ready."

"Are you sure you want to end your trip early? I can just drive them over," Hank said.

Peggin shook her head. "Not a good idea without me there. Whisper Hollow…the town has her own rules and ways. Ari, if you can run back to your place with me, we can head out from there."

Hank jumped up. "I'm good. I'll probably stay in Port Townsend for the night." He turned to Tad. "I won't be in tomorrow."

"Sounds good," Tad said. "Text us and let us know when you get there, and when you're settled into a hotel."

I turned to Elsbet. "I hope you're safe there, and…I hope you have a good life." I wasn't sure what else to say. We had come to the end of the road on this one.

Tabitha and Zoey drove off. Then, Elsbet made her good-byes—short and sweet, and altogether odd—and she followed Hank out to his SUV. As he helped her and the baby in, I wondered if they would be safe, and what would become of them.

Peggin said good-bye, too, and we traded phone numbers before she and Ari headed out. Caitlin left as well, and finally, just Teran and me, and Killian and Tally were there.

I turned to them, feeling like the world had shifted around me. We had found our way into a different realm. I had learned more about the world of Faerie than I had expected to—or wanted to know.

The longer I worked for Conjure Ink, the more I was finding that the world was far more than it appeared to be. Even though I had known all about shifters and vamps and—of course, witches—there were so many other mysteries hiding right in plain sight. As I locked the front door and returned to the living room, I couldn't help but wonder what would be coming at us next. And would we be able to handle it?

CHAPTER SIXTEEN

"So…" I wasn't sure what to say, so much had happened.

"Sit down and rest," Killian said, patting the sofa beside him.

I wandered over, feeling oddly at a loss, and then settled down beside him, leaning into his embrace. "Thank you, and you too, Tally, for coming after us. I don't know if we would have been able to escape."

Teran stood and stretched. "I'm going to forage through your cupboards to see what you have to eat. I think we've all used more energy than is good for us tonight."

I glanced over at Tally. "You're a beautiful wolf."

She grinned. "It felt good. I do much better in my alt-form, and I needed a good run. Besides, our parents taught us to never let the bullies win."

Killian excused himself to go to the bathroom. As soon as he was out of the room, Tally turned to me. "I know you thought I was some other wolf shifter—I'm sorry I didn't have a chance to warn you about that."

I blushed. "Was I that obvious?"

"It's no shame to be territorial with your man. You'll see a lot of that if you stick around. My family left our original Pack when we moved up here, but we joined the Rainier Wolf Pack—a local group of progressive wolf shifters. But regardless of how progressive we are, I can tell you right now, wolf shifters will forever be territorial. We respect the Alpha and Bitch of the group, and we band together. One nice thing about being a wolf shifter, unless you're rogue, there's always going to be someone to help you out when you need it, whether it's babysitting, moving, or repairing things around the house. We look after our own. The elderly never are left to fend for themselves. Everybody eats—if you don't have enough, the Pack will help you pull through."

I nodded, thinking that it sounded nice. Having a community was a wonderful thing. Witchblood families weren't quite so caring of one another, and humans seemed to have forgotten what extended family meant— at least in a general sense.

"What happens if someone's out of work for a long time and can't pay their mortgage?"

"Most Packs require a tithe every month and it goes into a general fund. Every working member contributes. Then, if someone needs help, they can petition for support, if they can't get regular unemployment. They are expected to put in community service hours in exchange. Most who need to go that route also repay as best as they can once they have secured a new job and gotten back on their feet, though it's not required."

I glanced down the hall at the powder room door. "Will Killian join your pack?"

"Probably, since the rest of his family is part of it. Generally, Pack members try to live within a certain territory, but exceptions are made. You can move a long distance and stay with your pack, but there's a disconnect that happens from not seeing the other members on a regular basis."

Teran popped her head around the corner. "Come into the kitchen. I've made us a snack."

When Teran said she had made a snack, what she meant was that she threw together a tasty meal, rather than just opening a few bags of chips. And true to form, when Tally and I walked into the kitchen, there were bowls of hot chicken soup on the table, along with grilled cheese sandwiches.

"It's canned—the soup. I didn't have time to make it from scratch. But I added a few herbs and spices and also some shaved carrots and diced celery to give it extra body. But the sandwiches have both aged cheddar and gouda in them, and everything is piping hot."

Killian joined us then, licking his lips as he stared at the food. "I'm hungry. Running around in my alt-form always gives me an appetite." He paused. "I hear Xi mewing."

"Oh, for heaven's sake." I jumped up. "I forgot to let them out of the guest room. Now that everybody's gone, it's safe." I headed for the stairs, realizing that my muscles ached from being out in the cold and rain all evening.

I leaned heavily on the railing. I really did need to find a gym. I'd never be in top-notch shape, but I wanted to have more endurance and stamina. As I opened the door and watched Klaus and Xi tumble out, my phone sounded. I pulled it out and saw it was a text from Ari.

PEGGIN AND HANK TOOK OFF ABOUT FIFTEEN MINUTES AGO, WITH ELSBET AND THE BABY. I SURE HOPE THEY'RE DOING THE RIGHT THING. I KNOW ELSBET HELPED US, BUT I CAN'T HELP BUT WORRY.

I texted back: I KNOW. I THOUGHT ABOUT THAT TOO, BUT THERE'S NOTHING WE CAN DO NOW. WE'LL JUST HAVE TO WAIT UNTIL HANK TEXTS US THAT EVERYTHING IS OKAY. AT LEAST HE'S DRIVING THEM AND NOT PEGGIN. I LIKE HER, BY THE WAY.

I LIKE HER TOO. I WAS A LITTLE WORRIED THAT MAYBE I REMEMBERED THE TRIP TO WHISPER HOLLOW TOO FONDLY, BUT I WASN'T DISAPPOINTED. WE SHOULD TAKE A TRIP OVER THERE IN THE SUMMER AT SOME POINT. AUTUMN'S TOO SPOOKY TO GO THERE.

I texted back good night, telling her I'd call her tomorrow, then returned to the kitchen. Xi and Klaus were chowing down. Killian had given them their gooshy food for dinner and they were falling over one another, nudging each other out of the way as they shifted places at the food bowl.

We gathered around the table to eat, talking over and around the evening, but none of us felt like revisiting the trip through the woods. So we talked about Tally's upcoming return to her work—the doctor was clearing her to return to her job.

"I'm thinking I might want to go back to school, though," she said.

"You didn't tell me that," Killian said, looking at her. "What do you want to study?"

"I'd like to train as a medical records technician. They

make good money, you can work remote if needed for some places, and it sounds interesting." She paused, then cleared her throat. "Did I tell you I'm dating again?"

That took Killian by surprise. He jerked his head around and I could instantly feel his protective nature rear up. "Who?"

"Les Howling Moon. He's the assistant to the Pack shaman."

Killian slowly put down his spoon and wiped his lips on a napkin. "What do the folks say about this?" He was giving her a look that made me slightly nervous. Watching the pair of them, I was getting a good lesson in Pack hierarchy.

"Mother invited him to dinner last week. He and Dad had a long talk. They gave their approval after he went home, so we're officially dating." She beamed at him and Killian visibly relaxed.

I cleared my throat. "Do you mind if I ask...do your parents have to approve of your dates?" I hadn't met Killian's parents. Did that mean we weren't officially a couple?

Killian glanced at me. "Within the Pack, yes. Outside of the Pack, it all depends. If Tally were to take up dating someone inside the Pack our parents didn't approve of, they could appeal to the Alpha to end the relationship. Given Tally's had one bad marriage, if they thought Les was problematic, then they probably would do just that."

"Your Pack is one giant family, blood-related or not, isn't it?"

Tally nodded. "You're beginning to understand how we work. Yes, we are like one massive family. Each household, the parents—or whoever's in charge, if the person is single—is considered the Alpha of that home. But over the entire Pack, the Alpha and his Bitch have the final word. We have a council of elders, and if someone disagrees with the rule of the Alpha they appeal to the council. The case is heard. Both parties agree to abide by the rule of mediation—in essence, the council. But that doesn't happen often, and usually if someone reaches that stage, they just leave the Pack instead."

"I'd like to understand my family more," I said. "I just found my great-grandmother's diary and I've started reading it."

"Witchblood families are united, but the only court we answer to is that of our guild—if we belong to one—and the Court Magika, who rules over every witch, every-where," Teran replied.

"That reminds me, I need to check my email," I said. "I approached the Court Magika the other day about Elli-son." I turned to Tally. "My ex threatened me the other night."

"If that happened in the Pack, the Alpha would have his hide," she said. "That's what happened to my ex. He was cast out when they found out what he was doing to me."

I pulled out my phone and checked my email. I usually glanced over it every day, but the past few days, I had been so busy that I had forgotten. Sure enough, there was an email from the Court. I opened it.

Dear Ms. Jaxson:

The Court Magika has found that Ellison Reilly presents a great and certain threat to you, January Jaxson, his ex-wife. As you are a certified member of the witchblood community by your parentage, we will send him one warning to stay away from you. If he breaks that warning, we will retaliate. Please make an appointment to talk to High Priestess Saturina Monet, who will walk you through all of the steps.

Sincerely,

Savon Crenshaw, Legal Counsel

"Well, that was fast." I read them the note. "So, Ellison better watch his step." As I was glancing through the string of emails, I found one from the Aseer, who wanted to see me the next morning—which meant I'd have to take the morning off, if not the entire day. I dropped a line to Tad. Then I found an email from the Moonshadow Bay Courthouse. It stated that my restraining order against Ellison had been granted and I was to pick up a copy of it as soon as possible and sign for it to be served to Ellison.

"Sounds like you have everything in hand," Teran said. "I still think you should steer clear of the Court Magika, but at least they have your back."

"I still want to visit Ellison and make certain he never darkens your door again." Killian stared at me, challenging me to tell him no.

Given what I had learned about the way his Pack worked—and the fact that they were progressive—I counted myself lucky that he hadn't bashed Ellison's head in. While I was grateful he cared enough to stand up for me, I was leery about controlling men.

"Well, the incident is being taken care of," I said, yawning. I had finished my soup and sandwich and the day was taking its toll. "I need to sleep," I said. "I'm going to kick all of you out and go to bed."

"Even me?" Killian said, batting his eyelashes.

Laughing, I leaned over and gave him a smooch on the nose. "Even you, love. Go home, get some rest. Tomorrow's a work day and regardless of what we accomplished tonight, we all have work to do."

Tally and Killian left via the kitchen door. Killian had installed a gate in the fence between our yards, and as I waved at them, I happened to glance at the Mystic Wood. The aura of the wood was lit up like fireworks. I watched, feeling creatures watching back. But the curtain of protection I had erected between the forest and my yard was holding, and after a nervous moment, I returned inside to find Teran still sitting in the kitchen.

"We need to have a talk," she said. "You said you're going in to see the Aseer tomorrow?"

I nodded. "Yes. I'm not sure what to expect, but you and Ari and just about every witch in Moonshadow Bay has been through the test, so I'm not necessarily that worried."

"Nor should you be. It's a bit invasive—but if you put aside your fears and open up, the test will only take a short time and then you'll know which direction to focus your study in. While most of us who are witchblood can learn the basics of protection and warding and other necessary life spells, almost every member of the magical community has a certain proclivity for one particular element. Like the owners of the Besom & Broom. They're aquanistas."

"Right. There are a few, though, who can work with all elements, correct?"

She nodded as she stood up. "Yes, and then there are the healers, the druids, the shamans—like Peggin's friend, the spirit shaman. There are many variations in magical folk, but most of the witchblood tend to be focused on elemental magic."

I yawned again and looped my arm through Teran's, walking her into the living room. "If we're going to talk, let's be comfortable. Do you want to stay the night?"

She shrugged. "It's a quick hike back to my place, so no. I'll make it quick, though. When you go to the Aseer, you'll have to tell her that your grandmother is Rowan Firesong. Otherwise, she may not look for particular traits and gifts."

I hadn't even thought of that. "Rowan may not like that—"

"Rowan can blow it out her ass. This isn't her call. This isn't her life. She made the choice not to tell your father and I think she did him a grave disservice. But you need to have all the information you can. Going to the Aseer later in life can be a little overwhelming."

"Does it happen often?" I asked.

"Usually only in cases where someone's an orphan and they didn't realize they had witchblood until they grew up. Your mother was a freethinker, in many ways. She wanted you to develop on your own as much as possible. If she would have taken you in when you were little, she would have had to explain about Rowan, and that would have been even more awkward." Teran scooped up Klaus, who was crawling up her pants leg. "Hello, cutie."

I sat on a cushion near the fireplace, bringing my knees to my chest and wrapping my arms around them. "What do you think of Killian?"

Teran blinked, looking startled. "Why do you ask?"

"You're my aunt. I trust your judgment. And you see through people. I'm in love, Auntie, and I know I'm not always the best judge of character. What Killian was saying tonight about his parents appealing to the Alpha if they didn't approve of Tally's beau…that kind of threw me."

Teran chuckled, stretching out on the sofa. "I think what threw you more is that he hasn't introduced you to them. Even though I know you're not really looking forward to that meeting, I noticed that when he was talking about the parents' approval making it official, you seemed taken aback."

I ruminated on what she said, then nodded. "I suppose you're right. We've said 'I love you'… Does that mean those feelings would be instantly negated if his parents don't approve of me? Could they break us up?"

Teran frowned, then propped her head up with her hand. "I suppose they could. But if you want my opinion, I think they're less likely to do that to their sons. Shifter culture, with a few exceptions, can be very patriarchal and even though the Rainier Wolf Pack is considered progressive, you have to figure that means progressive *as far as wolf shifters go*."

I nodded, hugging my knees to my chest and resting my chin on them. "Why didn't you ever marry? Have you ever been in love?"

Teran paused, as though debating what to say. Then, she let out a long sigh and sat up, crossing her legs as she leaned back on the sofa.

"Here's the thing. My mother—your grandmother Naomi—was all about independence for women. She said her mother had been saddled with so many kids that she had never had a chance to live up to her full potential. I'm not sure what you've read in Colleen's diary so far, but your grandmother used to talk about how bitter Colleen had been over being stuck at home. Colleen loved her children, but she wasn't cut out to be a mother. But back then, even among magical folk, birth control was hard to come by, illegal in most cases, and apparently Grandpa Brian wanted a houseful of kids."

I nodded. "Colleen loved her kids, though—at least from the entries I'm reading."

"Oh, you can love someone and yet find them a burden. Most people would feel too guilty to admit that, but it's true. Anyway, my mother brought Althea and me up to be independent. She made sure we went to college. She made certain we felt like we were good enough on our own. My father—your grandpa Campbell—pretty much ignored us except when we got into trouble."

Grandpa Campbell had died three years before I was born, but I remembered Grandma Naomi clearly. She still emailed me now and then, all the way from Ireland, demanding to know all about what I was doing. She had moved the year I was eight. I had both loved and feared Grandma Naomi. She was imposing, fierce even, and no nonsense. But I had never felt overlooked by her, and she made it clear that she expected my best behavior because she believed in me.

"I remember one time when I was six when we went to visit her. She lived down on…what was it? Violet Avenue?"

"Yes, she had that little cottage," Teran said. "She sold the house Althea and I grew up in, because she said it was far too much house for one person to manage."

"I remember she always kept the cottage neat as a pin. We went to visit her one Saturday for dinner and she bundled me into the kitchen, wrapped me in an apron that was too big for me, and then we made biscuits and fried chicken together. Or rather, I helped her make the biscuits and kept her company while she fried up the chicken. She sent Mom out to weed the garden and she asked Dad to mend a few things around the house."

Teran laughed. "My mother could always put anybody to work and make them glad to be helping. She just has a way about her."

"Well, we were talking, and she asked me what I wanted to be when I grew up. I told her a writer, and she nodded, very seriously, and told me that if I was going to be a journalist, I'd better make sure of my ethics because once you destroy someone in print, they'll never shake the reputation you give them. I never forgot that."

"That sounds like her," Teran said, looking misty. "I miss her. I really do."

"How old is she now?" I asked.

"She'll be one hundred next year. She's going strong, though. Our family blood lives well toward 150. She still gets out with the Audubon Society on bird walks, and the Sierra Club on environmental hikes." She sighed. "Maybe I should take a trip over to visit her. She hasn't been back here since 2012. That's quite awhile."

"So, why didn't you ever marry? Was it just Grandma Naomi teaching you to stand on your own two feet?"

Teran shook her head. "No, actually. I almost got married one year—I was twenty-three. His name was Caine Rodgers. And he was fine. He was handsome and rugged and from a druidical family. He knew the Mystic Wood like the back of his hand."

She had a dreamy look on her face, one I had never before seen when she talked about men. But it was also melancholy, and so I prepared myself for some tragic love story that she never recovered from.

"What happened?" I asked.

Teran paused, frowning. "I'm not sure whether to tell you."

"What? You can't leave me hanging! What happened?"

She sighed again. "You have to promise me that you won't hold this against her."

"Her who?" I asked.

"Promise me. You have to trust me," Teran said.

I finally nodded, giving her my promise. "What happened?"

"The same thing happened to me that your great-grandmother feared might happen with Brian. Rowan Firesong slept with my fiancé. She slept with Caine, and I found out."

I groaned. My grandmother was turning out to be quite the homewrecker. "But she's…"

"Older? Yeah, but she's still a handsome woman, even now. And her family is very long-lived. She was a beauty in her younger days—really stunning. And those days didn't end all that long ago. Anyway, she slept with Caine and then dropped him shortly after. That's one reason she and I aren't better friends. Oh, I've long let it go—I don't think I would have been happy with him in the long run, anyway. I love my life, and I got over it, after a while."

"Why did she do that to you?" Given how I had felt when I found Ellison cheating on me, I couldn't imagine why someone would willingly break up another relationship. I loved sex, but it wasn't that hard to find partners who were single, especially if you weren't out for a long-term connection.

"Rowan told me she was testing him, and he failed. I rather doubt that. But whatever the case, they slept together and that was it. I called off the engagement. Since then, I've never met a man I liked enough to settle down with." Teran shrugged, giving me a bittersweet smile. "The irony is, he was always the one afraid I'd sleep around. I was hard to pin down, even then, and it took him three proposals over five months for me to finally say yes."

"Well, that answers my question," I said, yawning again. "I'm sorry she did that."

"Me too, but then again, Caine had a choice. That's one thing I do know about Rowan, she's never used anything but seduction to gain a lover. She would never coerce anyone magically."

Teran stood up. "Enough old stories for tonight. I'd like to read that diary when you're done with it. Let me know what the Aseer says tomorrow."

I walked her to the door where she gave me a long hug. "I love you, sweetie," she whispered.

"I love you, too. Text me when you arrive home." I waved as she set out, then quickly shut out the night. Too many dangers lurked in the shadows and I didn't feel up to facing anything else tonight. Locking up and making sure my wards were holding, I headed upstairs for the night. But try as I might, I couldn't stop wondering what the Aseer's test would show. It was three A.M. before I managed to drift off to sleep.

CHAPTER SEVENTEEN

*T*he next morning, I dressed with extra care. While I knew this wasn't a formal interview, like for a job, the thought that I was going to be testing with the Aseer loomed large in my mind. I went for stretch jeans—I didn't know if I'd be asked to do anything athletic—and paired them with a V-neck sweater in plum. A silver chain belt around my waist and a pair of ankle boots completed the look. Sweeping my hair back into a ponytail, I felt ready to face the world.

A text came through from Killian. GOOD LUCK AND GO KNOCK 'EM DEAD, LOVE.

I texted back a mournful I'M SCARED…to which he replied like a good boyfriend should.

BUCK UP AND FACE YOUR FEAR. IF THE ASEER IS MEAN TO YOU, I'LL HAVE HER FOR LUNCH.

Laughing, I shot back, I LOVE YOU, and stuck my phone in my purse. As I locked the door behind me, after making sure the wards were still strong, it occurred to me that today could well change the direction of my life. I had no idea what was going to happen, but Esmara whispered to me as I clattered down the stairs, heading for my car.

You'll do fine, but you're going to learn more about yourself than you ever guessed. I'll enjoy seeing what happens.

Great, I countered back. *That feels like telling someone "May you live in interesting times." More of a curse than a blessing.*

Take it as you will, Esmara said. *But there's no getting away from destiny.*

With that warning ringing in my ears, I headed toward the Aseer's.

THE ASEER LIVED IN A SMALL COTTAGE ON THE SHORE OF the bay. As I drove up, I was surprised to see that the high tide almost reached her front porch steps. That was probably why her house was built up on stilts. The foundation was well above the surface of the beach. Wondering just how sturdy it could be, I parked by the sedan in the driveway and walked out on the beach for a moment, to stare at the water rushing in.

The tidal influences were strong in the Salish Sea. Connected to the Pacific Ocean by the Strait of Juan de Fuca, the Salish Sea was a recent name given to the bodies of water that surrounded the islands off the coast of Washington and British Columbia. Those same waters flowed into Puget Sound, creating the massive waterway that fingered its way all the way down to the Tacoma area, and even down into the bays of Olympia.

As I stood there, the wind bracing me up with cool, chill gusts that whipped by, a flock of seagulls few overhead, their mournful cries echoing through the air. The smell of seaweed hung heavy in the air, but it was the smell of home to me. I watched the water for a while, feeling the waves swell up as they rolled onto the shore.

"Hello." The voice echoed down from behind me and I turned to see a woman standing on the deck of the beach house. She might have been forty, might have been sixty, might have been almost any age in the world. She was what they called *timeless*. Ageless in that way some women have about them. She wore her years like a shroud, but instead of weighing her down, they surrounded her like a glamour. "Are you January?"

I nodded, shading my eyes as I looked up at her. "Yes, are you the Aseer?"

"I am. Come up. There will be rain soon, and the water can get testy when it rains." She waited for me as I climbed the steps up to the deck, then followed her into the house. The entire wall that faced the water was made of windows and sliding glass doors, and when I entered the house and turned, I caught my breath at the spectacular view.

"This must be beautiful when it's storming," I said.

"It's truly incredible, yes. In ten years I may have to move if the climate shifts too much, but until that day, I will stay here and watch over my beloved ocean." She nodded for me to follow her into the living room. "Please, have a seat."

She seemed far less imposing than I had expected, and yet there was something about her that warned me never to mess with her. She had power enough so that she didn't have to keep it on display.

The living room was very beachy—with an ivory sofa,

a blue wing chair, a driftwood coffee table and end tables. Even the console table standing against one wall was made of driftwood. I looked around. The place felt light and airy, the walls were painted pale blue, and the ceiling, a soft white. There were lots of crystals and shells around, but they didn't feel overwhelming or kitschy. High over the living room was a loft, reached by a stairwell against the back wall. One archway led to the kitchen—I could see the table and stove from where I stood. Three other doors on the opposite side probably led to bedrooms and a bath.

"You have a lovely place," I said. "It seems roomy, too."

"It is, actually. It's bigger than it seems because of the layout and open concept." She headed toward the kitchen. "Would you like some coffee?"

"Yes, please. I wasn't sure whether to eat or drink before coming," I said, settling down on the sofa.

"Here you go," she said, returning with a coffeepot and mugs on a tray, along with a plate of cookies. "It's not like having bloodwork done. Eating won't interfere with the test." She settled down and poured our coffee. "Cream? Sugar?"

"Both, thank you. Lots of cream and one sugar." I looked around, wondering what to say. I didn't even know her name beyond her title. "What…should I call you? I'm very unfamiliar with this. I left home without being tested and spent eighteen years ignoring my powers."

"It's a wonder they didn't overload and blow your brains out," she said, as nonchalantly as she might have said "Look at that water" or "Wow, it's windy today."

I blinked. "That can happen? I heard it can happen to spirit shamans, but I'm witchblood."

"Oh, it can happen to those who are witchblood as well." The Aseer sat back, crossing her legs. "As to my name, when I took the post of Aseer, I gave up my own name. Much like the druids and the post of the Merlin, the post of the Aseer is the title worn. So you may just call me 'Aseer.' It became my name the day the post was bestowed on me." She smiled a secretive smile, then said, "Do you have any idea of how old I am?"

I shook my head. "You look...timeless. I really don't have a clue."

"I'm 470 years old. I was made an Aseer back in England, before I came to this country." She paused, picking up a remote. "Do you mind if I turn on the fire-place? It's a little chilly in here."

I had no clue what to say about her age, so I just said, "Not at all—it is a bit chilly."

She flipped on the fireplace and a long line of bright, cheery flames appeared. The heat rippling off of it was immediate and I slid along the sofa, toward the long modern fireplace.

"That feels good," I said, closing my eyes. But a crackle of lightning startled me and I turned around, staring out the window as hail began to fall. "I love thunder and light-ning," I said, standing up and walking toward the wall of windows. "It always feels like it clears the air. There's a clean feeling afterward, an energy that's just waiting to be used."

"You don't say?" the Aseer said, joining me. We stared out over the water as the lightning danced from cloud to cloud, thunder rumbling shortly behind it. "What about windstorms?"

I shrugged, entranced by the lightning. "Windstorms can be fun, but they bring down the trees and I always start worrying about trees coming down." I paused, then asked, "So, when do we start the test? I can tell you I'm a little nervous. I have no clue what to expect."

"Expect only what comes, and don't invest worry into the future." The Aseer set down her coffee mug on a coaster that was resting on a side table. "The truth? We've already begun. You're deep into my test now."

Startled, I turned to look at her. "What? But you haven't asked me to do anything."

"Tests aren't always about questions and exams. A test merely measures information. I've been watching your reaction to the water, to the lightning and the fire. I've been tuning into how those elements react to you. We'll begin the formal session in a moment. I'm going to lead you along on a guided journey. I'll put you under hypnosis, and when you come out, we'll know far more." She motioned to the sofa. "Take off your shoes and stretch out in whatever way is most comfortable."

"My aunt warned me to tell you...Rowan Firesong is my grandmother."

If the Aseer was startled, she didn't show it. "Noted and acknowledged," was all she said.

That she had already been watching me didn't really surprise me, even though I hadn't thought about it. I unzipped my ankle boots and set them to one side, then turned on my side as I lay down on the sofa so that I was facing the room.

"Close your eyes and take three deep breaths," the Aseer said.

I did as she asked, letting the last one trickle out slowly.

"Now follow my voice. Follow my voice to wherever it leads you. You're safe here, this is a protected space that is inviolate. Anyone you meet along your journey will be a safe contact—safe to talk to, to interact with, to show them your inner self."

As the Aseer continued to speak, I found myself getting dozy. My breathing slowed and the world began to fall away. Try as hard as I might, I couldn't keep myself focused. Before I knew it, I was standing on a path, staring at a forest that rested at the bottom of the slope.

I STOOD AT THE TOP OF THE SLOPE...

From where I was, I could see that the forest was vast, spreading out beyond my ability to see the end. It was dark, and moody, reminding me somewhat of the Mystic Wood, but I felt a pull to it and knew that I must enter. I was on a journey into the forest to meet someone who was waiting for me, but I wasn't sure who it was or what they wanted.

I suddenly found a walking stick in my hand, and began walking down the grassy slope, staring at the forest ahead. The sky overhead was partially overcast, but the sun was peeking out from the edges, heading toward twilight.

You can make it any season you want... The words echoed

in my mind and I decided to try it. I focused on the wind and the temperature dropped. Ahead, in the forest, the leaves on the deciduous trees began to turn color, shifting to glorious bronzes and reds and yellow. Like a filter rolling over the forest, shades of autumn replaced the green leaves, and the conifers of the forest became interspersed with the hues of early autumn. The air shifted and I could smell that certain tang that creeps in when autumn comes calling.

Before I realized it, I was at the bottom of the slope, standing at the mouth of the trailhead. It loomed ominous, darker than out in the open. Twilight fell earlier in the forests than it did on the open slopes. Taking a deep breath, I stepped onto the path. I knew I had to enter the forest, and even though I felt a certain sense of doubt, a veil of protection surrounded me.

The trail was smooth-going, with only a tree root here or there, or a fist-sized rock to bar the way. I easily stepped over them as I made my way through the trees. The sound of birds singing their evensongs filled the air and I stopped to listen, trying to pinpoint what kind of birds they were. As I waited, unable to make out most of the bird chatter, a low *hoooooooooooot* echoed through the woodland and I glanced up a tall fir to see a barred owl sitting there, clinging to a branch. She—and I could feel the owl was a female—stared at me, and as I watched her, she let out another low hoot, but this time I could under-stand her. She was welcoming me into the forest. I raised my hand, holding it out to her, and she bobbed her head, her wide eyes almost aglow. As she did so, I heard a soft voice say, *You may continue.*

I passed by the tree with the owl in it, heading deeper into the forest.

Overhead, through the tangle of branches, the sky darkened into twilight, and the first hints of starlight glimmered overhead. The forest shifted, a feral sense creeping out on all fours, running through the trees, through the rocks and plants and bushes and animals. The woodland was taking on a sentience that had been asleep during the lazy daylight, but now it was wide awake and watchful.

"Why am I here?" I asked, my voice ringing through the air, ricocheting from tree to tree and echoing off the stones and the ground in a dizzying timbre.

Continue walking, came the reply.

Sucking in a deep breath, I obeyed.

As night fell, I began to notice tiny lights twinkling in the forest all around me. They shimmered from the toadstools growing on fallen nurse logs, from the tips of the fern fronds, from the moss dripping off the old-growth timber like ancient beards. The lights filled the forest like I imagined fireflies did. I ran my hand over some of the moss hanging nearby but as I drew away, my fingers were covered with sparkles and I gasped. Bringing my hand up to my nose, I inhaled the scent of magic—a heady blend of all autumn scents combined, like a potpourri of cinnamon and cedar and fresh rain and apple pie and bonfires.

"What is this?" I asked, hoping for an answer, but none came. *Are you there?* I asked Esmara.

I am with you, but I cannot interfere, nor can I give you any answers on this journey.

Relieved that at least someone knew where I was, I began to move forward again. The path seemed to be growing more difficult. It was harder to push on and while I didn't feel tired, I felt as though I was trudging through a thick fog that felt like mud. And then, the fog was really there, and all around me was a wall of mist that arose, shimmering with the fairy lights.

I stopped, waiting, and then one light—a brilliant purple—detached itself from the mist and began to dance in front of me, moving forward.

Follow the light.

And so, I followed the light as it sparkled and rose and dipped and danced ahead of me. The fog began to thin out, and then, as quickly as it had come, it was gone.

I turned around, wondering where I was. There, to one side, was a beautiful pool—a grotto with cinder blocks surrounding it, and natural stone, and on one side was a place to kneel. Without asking, I knew what to do.

I walked over to the pool, and as I did so, my clothes vanished, replaced with a long silver gown. It draped around my curves perfectly, and the moonlight broke through the trees, surrounding me in light. I had never felt so beautiful in my life.

I knelt on the dais beside the pond and leaned forward, resting my hands on the outcroppings of the stone that seemed perfect for handholds. Then, as I looked into the water, a light shimmered within the pool, spreading through the sea-green water to illuminate it. I caught sight of my reflection and gasped. My features and my hair seemed to glow like the rest of the forest, and all around me, I could see the reflection of the moon and the stars, creating a backdrop so that it felt like I was hovering in space. As I watched, I felt an inner prompt and I whispered a chant that flowed off my tongue.

Reveal myself, unto me,

Show me whom I'm meant to be.
By earth and air, by fire and sea,
Reveal all, I beseech thee.

There was a pause, and then lightning filled the sky behind me, and the rumble of thunder rolled through me like an inner earthquake as the world split apart and I found myself on a high mountain, my feet grounded in the earth. I could feel the bones of the world around me, and I reached up to catch the lightning, which ricocheted down from the heavens to roll through me, waking every sense—waking my magic from a long slumber.

It was spring, and vines were wrapping around my feet, coiling up to hold me firmly grounded to the earth, and the grass stirred, and I could hear the blades whispering among themselves, and the trees began to sing as they woke from their long sleep…

And then it was summer, and everything was dancing as the earth renewed herself. The herbs of the garden began chattering and telling me what they were used for, and flowers rejoiced, budding out, spreading their seed.

Come the autumn, I could feel the trees settle down, preparing for their long sleep, and the harvest rolled in, as pumpkins were loaded onto trucks, ready for market, and the last of the harvest was tucked away to fill larders and shelves and the woods took on a quiet watchfulness.

And then winter arrived, and the garden slept, as the forests were cloaked in snow and silence, but still, the heartbeat of the earth echoed through the barren landscape, reminding us that she was built of bones and rocks, of crystal and roots reaching deep into the world.

For a moment, I thought I was done, but then the pool

shimmered once more and as I glanced into it, a skull stared back at me. It opened its jaw and words whistled out on the wind.

Bones from the earth will speak to you. Spirits who were once blood and bone and muscle will seek you out. You will walk parallel to the road into the Underworld, for you can speak to the dead, and they will hear you and answer.

As the skull faded, I once again found myself standing at the edge of the forest, ready to exit, and there was Druantia. She reminded me of the most beautiful wood spirit ever to live, and she held out her hands.

"You are my daughter," she said. "Could you imagine you would not be ruled by the element of earth? Go forth and plant your gardens and tend your yard, and find a way to make peace with the Mystic Wood, for you, too, belong to the woodland now. You are also a guide for the dead—they can speak to you, those beings who were once tied to the soil. My daughter, you have found your magic. Welcome home to Moonshadow Bay, where you belong."

And as her words faded away, I began to feel dizzy. Holding my head, I sat down on a nearby tree trunk, closing my eyes, and when the fog began to lift, I looked up...

...and found myself on the Aseer's sofa.

I sat up, very slowly. Everything seemed different, and yet everything seemed the same. I had found my magic. I was bound to the earth, connected to the soil and the forests and the woodlands. And yet...I was connected to the Underworld as well. Feeling more at peace than I had in many years, I slowly smiled, and the Aseer smiled back.

CHAPTER EIGHTEEN

"Welcome back," the Aseer said.

I yawned. Blinking, I glanced at the clock on the wall and realized that I had been out for over an hour. "I'm sorry I took a nap on your sofa!"

She laughed. "Oh, you weren't napping. You were out on the astral, January. You were a busy bee, I could tell. Well, did you find your element?"

I grinned at her. She knew very well what element had picked me—that I could already tell, but it was nice of her to let me start the conversation. I told her what happened.

"So, it seems as though the element of earth claimed me...but the skull..." I hesitated. "This doesn't mean I'm... well...what Peggin's friend is, does it? A spirit shaman?"

"No," the Aseer said. "Being a guide for the dead is different. It means you can hear them and see them, but that doesn't give you the power to send them over through the Veil. You are more of a medium, than anything, when it comes to the dead. You'll be able to pick up on hauntings, and spirits. They can talk to you, if they choose. This would be ideal for a ghost hunter, you know. You should have a better chance of exorcising ghosts when need be, but remember—this does not apply to astral beings. It's not the same as taking on a demon or any such thing as that."

I paused, then asked the question I had been dreading to ask. "I told you that my paternal grandmother is Rowan Firesong. My father never knew she was his mother. Does that play into matters any?"

The Aseer stared at me for a moment. "Your father tested out high in his range, but there was never anything to tell me he was from such a strong family. But that does explain why your magic is focused in *two* areas. Rowan is a powerful witch from a powerful heritage. You should ask her more about your lineage, because there are several tales back there that may come back to haunt you…literally. Your magic both with the element of earth and with spirits will be very strong, so be cautious what you focus on. Make certain of your ethics, lest your strength lead you down a dark path. Rowan may seem abrupt, but she has an honor code that she will not break."

I nodded, feeling like I was being handed the key to the candy store and being told to ration myself. But it was good advice and, having sensed how powerful Rowan was, I was determined to avoid any more mistakes like the wishcraft ceremony Ari and I had performed for my birthday. I was still feeling ramifications from that ritual.

"So, what next?" I asked.

"Ask your aunt Teran to teach you how to use herbs and how to work garden magic. Learn to coexist with the Mystic Wood—I sense a hesitation in you about the forest."

I wasn't sure whether to tell her about the Woodlings and what had gone down. I decided to wait and talk to Rowan about it. "And talking to the dead?"

"Since your element is that of earth, crystals are your forte. Rather than tarot cards, a crystal ball. You'll find you commune well with the world of crystals and that you will respond to their energy in a way you didn't expect. By all means, experiment with the cards, but your strength lies in using the bones and stones, the herbs and woods of this world. Flower essences—magical blends using essential oils—this is your niche." She handed me a piece of paper.

It was a certificate that I had undergone the test of the Aseer and had tested out in the categories of earth and mediumship. I had seen my mother's certificate, though I didn't recall ever seeing my father's.

"Thank you," I said, feeling like I had just passed some sort of test with honors. Though it had brought up even more questions that only Rowan could answer.

"I'm glad you came to me. January, your magic has been bottlenecked for a long time. You're going into peri-menopause, aren't you?"

I blinked. I hadn't expected that question. "Yes, why?"

"If you don't start using your magic on a regular basis, the shifting hormones are going to set off…quakes, you might call them. You have to have an outlet for the magic, so use it. Don't store it up, or you might find yourself neck-deep in chaos caused by the energy breaking loose on its own." She laughed. "And it's not use it or lose it."

Blushing, I shook my head. "Oh good heavens, well, that I don't need. I'll start up regular practice, because the last thing I need is more chaos in my life."

As she showed me out, the Aseer and I stood on her deck, watching the waves swell as they reached the zenith of the high tide.

"Why am I so pulled to the water, if my element is earth?" I asked her.

She leaned on the railing of her deck, overlooking the shore. "We're *all* pulled to the water. It makes up around 60 percent of our bodies. Water is the primal mother—the great womb of the earth—and we respond to her. Her tides are ruled by the moon, and so we respond to the moon. The Ocean Mother is vast and comforting, terrifying and beautiful. She's so nebulous and yet she can grind down the mountains and carve deep channels in the land."

I thought about her words, then nodded. As I returned to my car, I felt like I had been in the Aseer's presence a long time. And in some ways, I had. I had gone in January Jaxson, recently returned to Moonshadow Bay, and I had come out a part of the witchblood community, with answers about who I was and who I was meant to be.

THAT EVENING, TALLY, KILLIAN, AND ARI JOINED ME FOR dinner. I told them what I had found out at the Aseer's.

I had spent all afternoon thinking over what I had found out about myself, and starting to make plans. It was the perfect time to plant a garden, so I'd plan out an herb garden and a kitchen garden. There was plenty of room in the backyard to plant some fruit trees, and somehow… someway…I would try to strike up a deeper connection with the Mystic Wood. Meanwhile, I'd also start looking for a crystal ball, and I realized, and not for the first time, that I needed my own athame. Both my mother's and my great-grandmother's athames were beautiful, but they weren't made for me. I needed one I could steep in my own magic.

"So…herbs, crystals…that makes sense. But the mediumship part is a little spooky," Killian said.

I shrugged. "I knew I had that part in me. Rowan gets back next week, so I'm going to talk to her then about it. And…I still need to finish reading my great-grandmother's book of shadows. There are things in there I need to know."

Ari leaned back in her chair, staring at her plate. I had made spaghetti and she had just polished off her second helping. "I think we should go on a camping trip over at Mount Baker. You and Killian, Meagan and me, maybe your aunt? You can't get much closer to nature than that."

"That's a good idea," I said. "When it warms up a little bit." I turned to Tally. "So, Killian said you're heading home?"

She nodded. "Tomorrow. I've had fun but it's time to go home. I need to enroll in the community college—I decided to take night courses there. That way I can work my job and still get my medical records certification. I really enjoyed meeting you, January. And all your friends," she added, smiling at Ari. "Maybe Killian should bring you down to meet the folks soon." She gave Killian a playful nudge and he grunted, but then he broke into a wide smile.

"That's my sister's formal seal of approval, love," he said. "And I am more than happy to schedule a time for you to meet the 'rents."

"I think that sounds…both delightful and daunting," I said. My phone rang at that moment. I glanced at the caller ID. "Damn it. Ellison." I was about to let it go to voice mail, but Killian grabbed the phone out of my hand and answered.

"Listen to me, slimeball. If you ever bother my woman again, I will go full-wolf on you and you can guess what that means." He was practically crackling. He paused for a second, then added, "Rant all you like, but keep it to yourself. You've been served with the restraining order, so fucking abide by it, Ellison, or you'll be in a world of hurt." And with that, he hung up.

I stared at him for a moment. "My gods, you really…" I stopped. I had been going to chastise him for threatening Ellison without asking me, but what Tally had told me about the Pack had stuck, and I realized that Killian needed to express his concern for me in the best way that he understood. He was a wolf shifter, and he would never be fully domesticated. There would always be a wild side to him, and that expressed itself in his concern for his loved ones. I was part of his Pack, regardless of how I saw things.

"Really what?" he asked, holding my gaze.

I shook my head. "You probably threw him into a tailspin," I said, sidestepping the issue. "Anybody ready for dessert? I bought a lemon meringue pie."

And as I dished up dessert, I couldn't help but think about how drastically my life had changed over the past few months. As I mused on the gardens I would plant, Xi and Klaus came racing by. Xi skidded to a halt beside me and looked up, sending a massive rush of love and joy my way. She was starting to grow up. She was still young

—still a kitten—but she was growing into my familiar, and we would work wonderful magic together. Klaus sat down and started grooming his butt in front of everyone.

Laughing, I served the pie, grateful for my new life, and my new path. Both promised to be incredibly exciting.

Late that night, after Killian and Tally had gone back to his place, I padded into the library and turned on the light. I couldn't sleep, so I pulled out my great-grandmother's book of shadows and sat down, starting to read.

Colleen's Book of Shadows
Entry: May 8, 1924

And so it's been a year to the date since they found our blessed Lara. We're keeping her death quiet. Only the sheriff knows, besides Rowan and myself. And we've decided to just tell people that she wandered off into the forest and hasn't been heard from since.

The sheriff actually believes that, and so does Brian, thanks to Rowan and her friend, Val Slater. We're hoping they never remember that my daughter was murdered. Because to tell people that Lara was dead would mean that eventually, the truth about Lara's killer would come out. Given the circumstances, people would talk, and rumors don't die and this lovely town would never be the same.

I've never mentioned it, even here, because words can be damning, but I have to tell someone, and I keep this journal hidden away, so the time to put words to the truth is now.

Rowan and I know who killed Lara, and he will never again harm another child. Rowan helped me make certain that he'll never again breathe the air, walk upon the earth, warm himself by the fire, or soothe his thirst with cool water.

And only his grave deep in the Mystic Wood holds the truth, along with his skeleton. I left an account, sealed in a jar, should anyone ever find his resting place in the future and exhume his body. But as the gods are my witnesses, he was guilty of killing more than just my baby girl. So Rowan and I sought him out to make certain he'll never again touch another child. I feel neither guilt nor remorse. The only thing I feel is sorrow that we didn't find him in time to save my daughter.

But life goes on, and I will never again mention this. Rowan and I have taken a vow of silence. If she outlives me, she will do as she pleases, and vice versa…but yes…we who are of witchblood stick together. And women have always had stronger stomachs for doing dirty work than men, which is why we didn't bring Brian into it. And that is the way it will stay.

I stared at the pages, feeling something shift. As I slowly walked into the kitchen and out on the back porch, I realized just how strong the women in my family—both sides—were.

Out back, the Mystic Wood was lit up with a ghostly

aura that shimmered over it, as brilliant as the aurora borealis. And out there in the forest was a grave and in that grave, the remains of a murderer, and my great-grandmother's story of what she and Rowan did.

Someday, I'm going to go hunting for it, I whispered to myself. *Someday, I want to find it and read what happened.*

Or you can just ask Rowan, Esmara said, her words tickling my ears. *Before you do something that might not be undone, talk to Rowan and ask her for her story. You may otherwise regret your actions—they may set something dark into motion that you cannot control.*

With the past hanging heavy in my mind, I took a deep breath and returned inside, closing the door firmly behind me, mindful of Esmara's warning.

Yes, the past was a mystery that beckoned, but meanwhile I had my future to face, and gardens to plant, and friendships to nurture, and a budding relationship that was getting more serious every day. I had a job that I loved, and now…ghosts to meet and talk to, and spells to cast. And I was looking forward to every minute of it.

IF YOU ENJOYED **CONJURE WEB**, BE SURE TO READ **Starlight Web** and **Midnight Web**, the first two books in the **Moonshadow Bay Series**. You can preorder the next book in the series: **Harvest Web**. There will be more to come of January's adventures after that.

If you're curious about Peggin and the town of Whisper Hollow, where spirits walk among the living and the lake never gives up her dead, you can read **Autumn Thorns, Shadow Silence**, and **The Phantom Queen**.

Come join the darkly seductive world of Kerris Fellwater, spirit shaman for the small lakeside community of Whisper Hollow.

If you love urban fantasy and mythology, then you might want to read the **Wild Hunt Series**. Check out **The Silver Stag, Oak & Thorns, Iron Bones, A Shadow of Crows, The Hallowed Hunt, The Silver Mist, Witching Hour, Witching Bones, A Sacred Magic, The Eternal Return, Sun Broken, Witching Moon, Autumn's Bane, Witching Time,** and **Hunter's Moon.** You can preorder the next books in the series—**Witching Fire** and **Veil of Stars**—now.

If you like paranormal women's fiction, try my **Chintz 'n China Paranormal Mystery Series: Ghost of a Chance, Legend of the Jade Dragon, Murder Under a Mystic Moon, A Harvest of Bones, One Hex of a Wedding**, and a holiday novella: **Holiday Spirits**. You can preorder the next book: **Well of Secrets.**

If you prefer a lighter-hearted paranormal romance, meet the wild and magical residents of Bedlam in my **Bewitching Bedlam Series.** Fun-loving witch Maddy Gallowglass, her smoking-hot vampire lover Aegis, and their crazed cjinn Bubba (part djinn, all cat) rock it out in Bedlam, a magical town on a mystical island. **Bewitching Bedlam, Maudlin's Mayhem, Siren's Song, Witches Wild, Casting Curses, Demon's Delight, Bedlam Calling, Blood Music, Blood Vengeance, Tiger Tails,** and Bubba's origin story—**The Wish Factor**—are available.

I invite you to visit Fury's world. Bound to Hecate, Fury is a minor goddess, taking care of the Abominations who come off the World Tree. Books one through five are available now in the **Fury Unbound Series: Fury Rising,**

Fury's Magic, Fury Awakened, Fury Calling, and **Fury's Mantle.**

For a dark, gritty, steamy series, try my world of **The Indigo Court**, where the long winter has come, and the Vampiric Fae are on the rise. **Night Myst, Night Veil, Night Seeker, Night Vision, Night's End,** and **Night Shivers** are all available now.

For all of my work, both published and upcoming releases, see the Biography at the end of this book, or check out my website at **Galenorn.com** and be sure and sign up for my **newsletter** to receive news about all my new releases. And if you want to support me in other ways, I have a Patreon Page and I also have a YouTube Channel.

QUALITY CONTROL: This work has been professionally edited and proofread. If you encounter any typos or formatting issues ONLY, please contact me through my **website** so they may be corrected. Otherwise, know that this book is in my style and voice and editorial suggestions will not be entertained. Thank you.

PLAYLIST

I often write to music, and CONJURE WEB was no exception. Here's the playlist I used for this book.

- **Air:** Moon Fever; Surfing On A Rocket
- **Android Lust:** Here And Now
- **Arch Leaves:** Nowhere To Go
- **Asteroids Galaxy Tour:** The Sun Ain't Shining No More; Sunshine Coolin'; Major; Heart Attack
- **Band of Skulls:** I Know What I Am
- **Beck:** Qué Onda Guero; Farewell Ride; Emergency Exit; Think I'm In Love; Cellphone's Dead; Nausea; Broken Train; Where It's At
- **The Black Angels:** Don't Play With Guns; Love Me Forever; You're Mine
- **Black Pumas:** Sweet Conversations
- **Blind Melon:** No Rain
- **Brandon Fiechter:** Night Fairies

- **Broken Bells:** The Ghost Inside
- **Bobbie Gentry:** Ode to Billie Joe
- **Camouflage Nights:** (It Could Be) Love
- **Crazy Town:** Butterfly
- **D.J. Shah:** Mellomaniac
- **David Bowie:** Fame; Golden Years; China Girl; Let's Dance
- **Deuter:** Silver Air 1; Petite Fleur
- **Donovan:** Season Of The Witch
- **Eastern Sun:** Beautiful Being (Original Edit)
- **Fats Domino:** I Want To Walk You Home
- **Gerry Rafferty:** Baker Street
- **Gordon Lightfoot:** Sundown
- **Gorillaz:** Last Living Souls; Dare; Demon Days; Hongkongaton; Rockit; Clint Eastwood
- **Heart:** Magic Man; White Lightning & Wine
- **Jay Price:** Dark-Hearted Man; The Devil's Bride; Coming For You Baby
- **Jeannie C. Riley:** Harper Valley P.T.A.
- **John Fogerty:** The Old Man Down The Road
- **Johnny Otis:** Willy & The Hand Jive
- **The Kills:** Nail In My Coffin; You Don't Own The Road; Sour Cherry
- **Kirsty MacColl:** In These Shoes?
- **Lady Gaga:** Born This Way; Paparazzi; Poker Face; Paper Gangsta; Stupid Love
- **Ladytron:** Paco!; I'm Not Scared
- **Low:** Witches; Plastic Cup; Half Light
- **Mannheim Steamroller:** G Major Toccata; Crystal; Interlude 7; The Dream; Z-row Gravity
- **Matt Corby:** Breathe
- **Men Without Hats:** Safety Dance

- **Nancy Sinatra:** These Boots Are Made For Walking
- **Red Venom:** Let's Get It On
- **Robin Schulz:** Sugar
- **The Rolling Stones:** Gimmer Shelter; Little Red Rooster; The Spider And The Fly; 19th Nervous Breakdown; Paint It Black; Mother's Little Helper; Lady Jane; Miss You
- **Rue de Soleil:** We Can Fly; Le Française; Wake Up Brother; Blues Du Soleil
- **Sam the Sham & The Pharoahs:** Lil'Red Riding Hood
- **Screaming Trees:** Where the Twain Shall Meet; All I Know
- **Shriekback:** The Shining Path; Underwaterboys; Intoxication; Over The Wire; New Man; Go Bang; Big Fun; Dust And A Shadow; Agony Box; Putting All the Lights Out; The Fire Has Brought Us; And The Rain; Wiggle And Drone; Church Of The Louder Light; Now These Days Are Gone; The King In The Tree
- **Simple Minds:** Don't You
- **Snow Patrol:** The Lightning Strike/What If This Storm Ends
- **Suzanne Vega:** Blood Makes Noise; 99.9F°; Bad Wisdom; Solitude Standing; Straight Lines
- **Sweet Talk Radio:** We All Fall Down
- **Tamaryn:** While You're Sleeping, I'm Dreaming; Violet's In A Pool
- **The Temptations:** Papa Was A Rolling Stone
- **Tingstad & Rumbel:** Chaco

PLAYLIST

- **Tom Petty:** Mary Jane's Last Dance
- **Trills:** Speak Loud
- **The Verve:** Bitter Sweet Symphony
- **Vive la Void:** Devil
- **Zero** 7: In The Waiting Line
- **The Zombies:** Time Of The Season

BIOGRAPHY

New York Times, Publishers Weekly, and *USA Today* best-selling author Yasmine Galenorn writes urban fantasy and paranormal romance, and is the author of over seventy books, including the Wild Hunt Series, the Fury Unbound Series, the Bewitching Bedlam Series, the Indigo Court Series, and the Otherworld Series, among others. She's also written nonfiction metaphysical books. She is the 2011 Career Achievement Award Winner in Urban Fantasy, given by RT Magazine. Yasmine has been in the Craft since 1980, is a shamanic witch and High Priestess. She describes her life as a blend of teacups and tattoos. She lives in Kirkland, WA, with her husband Samwise and their cats. Yasmine can be reached via her Website at Galenorn.com.

Indie Releases Currently Available:

Moonshadow Bay Series:

Starlight Web
Midnight Web
Conjure Web
Harvest Web

The Wild Hunt Series:
The Silver Stag
Oak & Thorns
Iron Bones
A Shadow of Crows
The Hallowed Hunt
The Silver Mist
Witching Hour
Witching Bones
A Sacred Magic
The Eternal Return
Sun Broken
Witching Moon
Autumn's Bane
Witching Time
Hunter's Moon
Witching Fire
Veil of Stars

Chintz 'n China Series:
Ghost of a Chance
Legend of the Jade Dragon
Murder Under a Mystic Moon
A Harvest of Bones
One Hex of a Wedding
Holiday Spirits

Well of Secrets

Chintz 'n China Books, 1 – 3: Ghost of a Chance, Legend of the Jade Dragon, Murder Under A Mystic Moon

Chintz 'n China Books, 4-6: A Harvest of Bones, One Hex of a Wedding, Holiday Spirits

Whisper Hollow Series:
Autumn Thorns
Shadow Silence
The Phantom Queen

Bewitching Bedlam Series:
Bewitching Bedlam
Maudlin's Mayhem
Siren's Song
Witches Wild
Casting Curses
Demon's Delight
Bedlam Calling: A Bewitching Bedlam Anthology
The Wish Factor (a prequel short story)
Blood Music (a prequel novella)
Blood Vengeance (a Bewitching Bedlam novella)
Tiger Tails (a Bewitching Bedlam novella)

Fury Unbound Series:
Fury Rising
Fury's Magic
Fury Awakened
Fury Calling
Fury's Mantle

Indigo Court Series:
    Night Myst
    Night Veil
    Night Seeker
    Night Vision
    Night's End
    Night Shivers
    Indigo Court Books, 1-3: Night Myst, Night Veil, Night Seeker (Boxed Set)
    Indigo Court Books, 4-6: Night Vision, Night's End, Night Shivers (Boxed Set)

Otherworld Series:
    Moon Shimmers
    Harvest Song
    Blood Bonds
    Otherworld Tales: Volume 1
    Otherworld Tales: Volume 2
    For the rest of the Otherworld Series, see website at **Galenorn.com.**

Bath and Body Series (originally under the name India Ink):
    Scent to Her Grave
    A Blush With Death
    Glossed and Found

Misc. Short Stories/Anthologies:
    Once Upon a Kiss (short story: Princess Charming)
    Once Upon a Curse (short story: Bones)
    Once Upon a Ghost (short story: Rapunzel Dreaming)

Witch Ways

Magickal Nonfiction:
Embracing the Moon
Tarot Journeys